SON OF HELL

AN ALEX MASON THRILLER

DAVID ARCHER

BLAKE BANNER

RIGHTHOUSE

PRAISE FOR ALEX MASON

ALEX MASON THRILLERS

Odin (Book 1)
Ice Cold Spy (Book 2)
Mason's Law (Book 3)
Assets and Liabilities (Book 4)
Russian Roulette (Book 5)
Executive Order (Book 6)
Dead Man Talking (Book 7)
All The King's Men (Book 8)
Flashpoint (Book 9)
Brotherhood of the Goat (Book 10)
Dead Hot (Book 11)
Blood on Megiddo (Book 12)
Son of Hell (Book 13)
Merchant of Death (Book 14)

O war, thou son of hell,
Whom angry heavens do make their minister
Throw in the frozen bosoms of our part
Hot coals of vengeance!

William Shakespeare, Henry VI Act 5 Scene 2

PROLOGUE

THE BLACKNESS WAS IMPENETRABLE. THE CLOUD cover was dense and low, cutting out any moonlight or starlight. Deep inside the remote Russian countryside, several miles from the Ukrainian border, all that was visible was the faint glow of the town of Pavlovsk in the distance and the occasional dim light winking through invisible trees to the south.

Captain Eddy 'Spud' Walker saw the distant fan of light, followed a second later by the glow of headlamps. They disappeared as quickly as they had appeared, and he spoke softly into the microphone in his helmet.

"Visual, estimate a mile out. Stand by. Radio silence till my command."

Nothing changed in the blackness, but the stillness seemed more intense, the low clouds seemed heavier, the silence more acute.

Again the headlamps fanned above a hill, closer now, throwing a copse of trees into sharp silhouette. The fan faded, and a moment later, the headlamps glared, casting a halo around those same trees, highlighting for a moment the ribbon of blacktop that would bring those headlamps to where Spud and his SAS patrol were waiting.

Based on intelligence provided by Ukrainian commandos just a few hours earlier, the convoy was small, just two Land Rovers, one in the vanguard and one at the rearguard, escorting a heavily armored van. There would be ten men maximum. Even if they were well-trained special operatives, it seemed poor protection for such a valuable cargo as this was.

On the other hand, Spud told himself, the aim was probably to keep a very low profile, and the last thing Moscow would be expecting right now was an SAS patrol to be operating deep inside Russian territory—not just occupied Ukraine, but Russia itself.

Now a single bright light emerged from where the road came around a low hill. For a moment, it had the appearance of a spotlight, but then it split like a luminous amoeba, and a moment later, the six headlamps seemed to merge and split again as they swelled and drew closer.

Spud was aware of his heart pounding, but his mind was ice-cold, and no emotions stirred inside him. He waited where he lay, behind a large rock just twenty feet from the road, till the lead Land Rover was drawing level with him. Then he spoke in a quiet, matter-of-fact voice.

"Fire one and two."

Less than a second later, two tank busters erupted from the darkness on the far side of the road. The first punched through the driver's door of the lead vehicle and exploded inside the driver's belly, vaporizing him and his copilot and tearing the two men in the back seat into carbonized, unrecognizable pieces. Simultaneously, the second rocket erupted through the trunk of the rear vehicle and exploded at the exact center between the heads of the four soldiers, vaporizing their brains, tearing their bodies into shreds, and incinerating them. Of the ten men escorting the armored vehicle, there were two left.

The lead vehicle did a small leap, like a burning elephant doing ballet. It hit the road, swerved, and rolled. The rear Land Rover went up on its snout and fell sideways, By then, Spud was already running, covering the twenty or thirty feet that separated him from the armored truck with his rifle at his shoulder. At fifteen feet, with the driver and the co-driver visible in the light from the flaming truck, he opened fire, triple-tapping twice, and the armor piercing rounds tore through the bulletproof glass and thudded home, three in each chest.

At the rear of the truck, he could hear Ernie 'Boomer' Skinner blowing the rear doors, then, as he ran to the back, Billy 'Bones' Fletcher and Sergeant Scotty McTavish barking at the prisoners in the van.

"*Out! Come on! One two! One two! Move it! Move it!*"

He made it to the back as the four blinking, bewildered men were dragged out through the shattered doors.

"*Run!*" he said, and the four blades surrounded the four prisoners and began to run, pushing and dragging them as they went.

One of the prisoners spoke. His accent was Pakistani. He began to say, "Who are you—" but Spud cut him short.

"Be silent, or I'll shoot you."

They ran for half a mile until they reached the abundant

undergrowth along the banks of a river. Here they stopped, crouching low among the foliage. Scotty pulled a radio from his fatigues, and Boomer and Bones trained their weapons on the prisoners. Spud produced a small key and spoke to the men.

"You all speak English?" They nodded. "Listen carefully and do not speak. You were being taken to a prison south of Moscow. There you were going to be tortured, tried for war crimes, and executed. We have liberated you, and you will come with us. I am going to remove your handcuffs. We will not hurt you, but if you try to escape, we will shoot you dead instantly. Do you understand?"

They nodded and muttered that they did.

Moments later, they waded knee-deep across the river and began a steady jog west and south toward the Ukrainian border. After about half an hour, a soft thudding noise came to them, and a dark silhouette emerged from the blackness of the night. The stealth chopper banked slightly and came to hover just three feet from the ground. A soldier leaned out and one by one pulled the prisoners aboard. When they were inside, the SAS patrol scrambled in, and as the hatch slid closed, the chopper rose, turned, and with a muted thudding, started back toward the border.

Ten Russian casualties, three vehicles for the scrap heap, zero casualties on the homes side, four captives for interrogation: not a bad couple of hours' work.

He allowed himself a small smile as he gazed down at the trees skimming past just fifty or sixty feet below.

Mission accomplished.

ONE

"WHAT THE HELL HAVE THE SUNNI MUSLIMS GOT against Russia?"

Gallin turned and looked at me, then hunched her shoulders as if she was answering her own question with a 'How the hell should I know?' After making me complicit in her own ignorance, she turned back to Nero, who was watching her from an oak paneled corner at the Ben Franklin Club in DC. His expression was passive from under hooded eyes. He raised his cognac, sniffed it with his substantial aquiline nose, and sipped. As he laid down the balloon glass, Gallin said, "When was the last time any Islamic terrorist took the blindest bit of interest in Russia? Since when is Russia the great Satan?"

"You mean aside from when the Soviet Union invaded Afghanistan, Captain? That is what we are all wondering. The four men appear to be Sunni Muslims rather than the Shiite who are engaged against Israel and her allies these days."

Gallin arched a very fine eyebrow at him. "Israel has allies these days? You'll have to introduce me. I know Ben would like to meet them."

"Indeed, I take your point, but let us try to avoid digressing."

"I always digress. It's what my English teacher at high school used to say to me: 'Aila, you always digress.' She was Jewish. Her name was Gladys Goldstein. I thought it was a nice alliteration. Gladys Goldstein and Alliterating Aila."

Nero sighed quietly through that considerable nose, gazing at the white linen tablecloth. I thought I caught the twitch of a smile at the corner of his mouth, and that made me wonder if he was attracted to Gallin. It was hard not to be, and he was after all a man. Though sometimes it was easy to forget that.

I interrupted my own thoughts and said, "So the question is, what is it about Russia, immediately after Putin's reelection, that would make Sunni Muslim terrorists open fire on a crowded shopping mall at eleven o'clock in the morning and massacre fifteen people, mainly women and children?" Nero raised both eyebrows and gave a single, ponderous nod. Before he could open his trap and start pontificating at me, I went on, "And the answer is clearly 'Nothing.' So maybe we need to turn the question around."

Gallin picked up her glass of twenty-one year-old Bushmills and scowled at it. "Turn it around? How?"

"What is it," I said, "about Russia, immediately after Putin's reelection, that would make them want to be attacked by Sunni Muslims?"

Nero cleared his throat and regarded me from under a single arched eyebrow. "Occasionally, Alex, you say something that makes me think perhaps I was not wrong to mentor you. Sadly, not often enough, but this is indeed the question. The Shiite Muslims have absolutely no motive for attacking Russia, as Russia is supporting them and Iran in their war against Israel. The Sunnis, though historically enemies of the Shiites, diverge from them only in their beliefs regarding who should have succeeded Mohamed as Calif. Their pathological hatred of the so-called 'people of the book,' that is the Christians and especially the Jews, is equal to the Shiites', and they have as little motive to attack the Russians. On the contrary, they have every reason to support the Russians as enemies of the West and Israel, just like the Shiites. Therefore we need to ask, How would Russia benefit from such an attack *if she were to orchestrate it herself?*"

I drew breath, but Gallin, frowning, raised a hand to me. "Wait. So they can't use Shiites for the attack because Iran is predominantly Shiite and they are allies. But they can use Sunnis because the West can barely tell the difference— they're just Muslims—but Iran won't object because *they* are enemies of the Sunni."

"Correct."

"So how does a Sunni terrorist attack on a shopping mall in Moscow benefit Russia and Iran? Don't tell me! First of all..." She nodded a few times, then trailed off. "I don't know. I don't get it."

Nero drew a deep breath. "If you will allow me, Captain, I shall tell you. We have kept it from the media, but we won't be able to keep it much longer. Russia is set to blame MI6— more correctly the Secret Intelligence Service, the SIS—for the attack."

She screwed up her face. "*What?*"

"It is not as mad as it sounds. The United Kingdom has longstanding good relations with several countries with predominantly Sunni populations and aristocracies. Besides which, after decades of neglecting what was once one of the finest armies in the world, Britain now has vastly depleted armed forces, and the British Ministry of Defense seems more concerned with making them 'inclusive' rather than effective. They have worked so hard at embracing diversity that their MoD no longer knows whom they are supposed to be defending and who is the enemy. So the last thing the British government wants right now is an armed conflict."

"So if Russia comes out accusing the UK of an act of war," Gallin interjected, "with the UK armed forces depleted and neither the US nor the EU with much stomach for a war with Russia, that could drive a stake right through the heart of NATO."

"Precisely, and though Israel is not a part of NATO, she has close military alliances with the most important members, such as the USA and the UK. But the consequences run deeper: With the man who will probably be the next president of the USA threatening to pull out of NATO, the UK virtually incapable of delivering a workable military force, and the EU overtly supporting Palestine, Israel's position becomes suddenly very vulnerable to Iran."

Gallin sagged back in her chair. "Jesus..."

Nero nodded as though he agreed with her. "Against that backdrop, it seems that Russia intends to rely on documentary evidence and witness testimony to prove, at the United Nations and at the International Court of Justice in the Hague, that the Secret Intelligence Service—MI6—

recruited these men to commit this atrocity, with the full knowledge of the British Government. Ostensibly with a view to damaging relations between Russia and the Muslim world, in particular Iran. So it is of the utmost importance that we stop that evidence from reaching the United Nations or the International Court of Justice."

"How are we going to do that?" I asked.

"You fly to London tomorrow, and then from Brize Norton tomorrow night to a British base of operations just to the east of Pisochyn, in eastern Ukraine, a few miles from the Russian occupied area. Acting on intelligence received from within the Russian military high command and Ukrainian commandos, the SAS were able to intercept a small convoy that had come by road from Tehran via Armenia and Georgia, headed for Moscow. Let us be thankful that this is one regiment at least that still prioritizes the defense of the United Kingdom over creating a welcoming space for a broad variety of extremists.

"There were two Land Rovers in the convoy, escorting an armored vehicle in which there were four prisoners. All four are Arab males, probably Sunni, though that is not confirmed. One of them is British Pakistani, one is from Iraq, one is French of Syrian origin, and the other is of Libyan origin. These men claim they were arrested in Iran and charged with the attack on the Russian shopping mall."

Gallin was shaking her head. "Wait, I thought we said the attack on the mall was not carried out by Iranians."

Nero nodded. "The story is they escaped from Russia through Georgia and Armenia and attempted to pass themselves off as Iranian Shiites. However, the Iranian police detected suspicious behavior and arrested them. Under interrogation, they confessed to their crimes, and the Iranian government sent them back to Russia."

She was still frowning. "They couldn't fly them? What is that, two thousand miles from Tehran to Moscow?"

Nero spread his hands. "Precisely. These are issues which I find interesting, and so you will fly to where they are being held and interrogate them. You will liaise there with George Locke, the SIS officer in charge of the investigation."

"Why us?" I asked. "This is a British issue." But even as I asked it, I was seeing the answer. Nero put it into words.

"In the first place, whatever internal crisis may be affecting Britain's army, its intelligence services are still second to none. So this affects the Five Eyes directly, and it also poses a tremendous threat to the integrity of NATO. It is hard to tell with Mr. Trump how much of what he says is bluster and how much he is actually prepared to see through to the end. But if Russia is not stopped, it could provide the final straw to make the future president say, 'NATO is no longer a benefit to America.'

"There is also the fact that there are many in the British administration who are fighting to restore Britain as a powerful, independent nation. But if the SIS is allowed to investigate this alone, Russia can easily allege that the criminal is investigating his own crime. So we need the investigation conducted by an independent third party."

I nodded. "Makes sense."

"Thank you," he said with a touch of irony and hooded eyes. "Go there, interrogate those men, and if necessary, bring them back to DC. I want to know if they were the actual perpetrators, and if so exactly who employed them, briefed them, and paid them."

. . .

OUT IN THE PARKING LOT, Gallin stood staring at my TVR Griffith. It is probably the most beautiful car in the world, and mine is burgundy, which elevates it to an even higher level.

I watched her face for a moment and said, "You're dribbling."

She turned and stared hard into my face. "Let me drive it."

"No." I shook my head and moved around the hood to the driver's door.

She leaned on the roof. "Let me drive it and I'll sleep with you."

I snorted in a derisive way and opened the door. "Why would I want to sleep with you?"

I climbed in behind the wheel, and she got in beside me. She was frowning.

"I have slept with you many times, Gallin." The engine growled, then roared, and we took off toward my house on Adams Street. "I can't say it has been unpleasant. You don't snore. You don't thrash or kick or talk in your sleep. You *certainly* don't keep me awake. But"—I gave a harsh laugh—"I really can't say it's an inducement to let you drive my car, either."

She had watched me quietly while I spoke. Now she said, "You're an asshole, Mason. I'm fond of you. I will always be your friend. But you are a first class asshole."

"If you knew, Gallin, how many people have said that to me."

We drove in silence for a while. Then she said, a little

ambiguously, "This could get pretty wild." I glanced at her. She said, "The key to power, Mason, is the ability to project violence to your farthest outposts. Two countries have been key to America's ability to do that since the Second World War: Britain and Israel. If Russia succeeds in this stupid plan, it could destroy that alliance." She gave a brief shrug. "The consequences for the States would be minimal. America is entering an introspective phase anyway, and it's protected on both sides by vast oceans. To some extent, Trump is right. America doesn't need NATO."

"I'm not sure that's true, Gallin."

"The consequences for Britain could be severe. The Muslim population there is growing at a tremendous rate, and the potential for civil unrest, even a coup, is becoming a reality. But for Israel, Mason, for Israel we could be looking at total annihilation. We are looking at the atrocities perpetrated on the 7th of October carried out on a national scale, against millions of people. Nobody seems to realize that, or if they do, they don't care."

I was quiet a while as I drove. When I spoke, it was half to myself. "The world is changing suddenly and violently. Nobody could have expected this, even twenty years ago. The incredible rise of evil, the collapse of old friendships and alliances..."

I trailed off, and Gallin snorted. "That famous New World Order Bush was so fond of talking about, it crumbled when Putin marched into Ukraine, but it was obliterated when Hamas raped and murdered men, women, and children in the streets of Israel, and her allies stood and watched, and blamed Israel. Welcome to the New World Order."

I nodded. "Yeah, this could get pretty wild." I took a

deep breath and sighed loudly. "Okay, you can drive my TVR Griffith to the airport tomorrow. I'll let you."

"Seriously?" She grinned.

"Does that mean you're going to sleep with me?"

"In your dreams! I still think you're an asshole." She shrugged. "You're just an asshole with a really nice car."

I heaved another sigh. "Manny Pacquiao warned me about women like you. I should have listened."

TWO

THE JOURNEY WAS LONG AND EXHAUSTING, FIRST
to London's Heathrow Airport, where we were met by an
RAF lieutenant in plain clothes who drove us north to the
Brize Norton airfield, where a jet was waiting on the tarmac
to take us on the three-hour, one thousand eight hundred
mile flight to the improvised military airfield at Pisochyn.
From Pisochyn, we were taken by chopper to where the
Siverskyi Donets river widens to some two miles and forms a
kind of lake beside Martove, near Chuhuiv. There, finally,
after fifteen hours of traveling, we arrived among the dense
woodlands that flank the river to where the SAS had their
operational command base, deep within the forest. It was
invisible from the ground and from the air. And also, it
didn't exist.

Officially, at least.

We landed on a comparatively flat field not far from the
river. The pilot twisted around and pointed to the trees that
sprawled over the banks fifty or sixty yards away. He raised

his voice above the thud and whine of the turbine and shouted, "*Head for the trees! Somebody will meet you!*"

We jumped down, hunched under the downdraft, and ran for the cover of the trees. As we approached, two guys in camouflage with assault rifles and green balaclavas stepped out. One of them snapped, "*Keep running!*" and fell in, one behind us and one in front. We kept running for maybe five minutes, following no particular path but dodging through the trees, like the guy in front knew where he was going.

Finally we entered a clearing, and the two troopers stopped. As they pulled off their balaclavas, it dawned on me that the clearing was flanked on four sides by large, camouflaged tents that were practically invisible.

The nearest of the guys approached and held out his hand.

"Captain Eddy Walker. We don't stand on ceremony here. People call me Spud."

As we shook his hand and gave him our names, another six men emerged from the undergrowth. Some were in military fatigues, others in jeans and sweatshirts. They all looked hard enough to break rocks with their teeth.

One of the guys in jeans approached, smiling. He had black hair, brown eyes, a moustache, and a pleasant manner. He looked Spanish, or Mediterranean, but Spud said, "This is George Locke, here from the Foreign Office. I believe you guys have stuff to talk about. We'll be around if you need us."

We shook hands with Locke, and he led us in among the trees again. After about twenty feet or a little more, we came to another large camouflage tent. He pulled back the flap, and we went in. There we saw four guys cuffed to chairs.

They didn't look happy, but they didn't look as though they'd been subjected to enhanced interrogation, either. They watched us with uncertain eyes.

George said, "This is your investigation, chaps. We need to prove that we were not involved in that massacre in Moscow. Obviously to do that, the intelligence must come from an independent observer. So I'll sit in on your interrogations, if I may, but I shan't be intervening." He gestured at the guy on the far right. He was clean shaven with short curly hair.

"This is Rashid Patel, from London and Pakistan." He pointed to the guy on his left who was sporting three large moustaches, one over each eye and one under his nose. "Mohamed Hussein, from Iraq." The guy next to him was clean shaven and practically bald. "Omar bin Abbas, French of Syrian origin, and finally the guy with the big beard is Hassan from Afghanistan—that's all he'll tell us. Perhaps you'll have more luck. Camp's moving out in a couple of days. Can't stay in any one place too long, you know. So we'd appreciate it if by then you knew exactly what you want to do with them."

It was Gallin who answered. "We'll know what to do with them by then, George."

He looked slightly surprised. "You're English? The MoD has specified they don't want English investigators—"

She cut him short, smiling down at Rashid, the English Pakistani guy. "I'm Israeli, George. I'm with the Mossad."

Rashid swallowed hard. George nodded and tried to conceal a smile. "Right," he said. "Good. So we have a little tent set off to one side over there, where you can take them one at a time."

Gallin was still smiling down at Rashid. "Is it sound-proofed?" George looked at me, his smile turning uncertain. Gallin grinned, still holding Rashid's eye. "I'm just kidding," she said like she really wasn't.

I nodded my head at Rashid. "We'll talk to Rashid first," I said. "I'm guessing you have mug shots of these guys?" He nodded. "I'll need those. You can send them to my phone."

"Will do. I'll have Rashid taken over. Meantime I'll show you your tent and your facilities. Pretty basic here, as I'm sure you'll understand."

We dumped our bags, had a wash, and met George ten minutes later at the interrogation tent. He stopped us outside and spoke in a quiet voice, looking at us both alternately but eyeing Gallin with caution.

"Look, I know there is a lot at stake here, not least for Israel, and I know that across the pond, you take a different approach to this kind of thing, but I really can't sanction what you guys call enhanced interrogation. That won't happen, not on my watch. Are we on the same page here?"

I glanced at Gallin. She nodded.

"We're on the same page. We need to be able to rely on any intelligence we get here, George, and we all know what you get under torture is not reliable." She shrugged. "What we do with them *after* the interrogation is another matter."

His face went hard, and his eyes were bright.

I said, "She's joking."

"Are you sure?"

"I'm joking, George. I have a twisted sense of humor. It comes with living with the daily risk of extermination. I'm not going to hurt your prisoners."

As she moved past him, she added, "I'm just going to try

and make them see the rainbow of joys that can spring from a free, inclusive world."

The last three words were directed at Rashid, who was sitting at a table in the middle of the tent. His wrists were manacled to a steel ring in the middle of the table, and his ankles were secured to his chair. There were two folding chairs opposite him for me and Gallin, and a fourth canvas chair was some six feet from the table to one side. George went and sat there. We sat opposite Rashid.

I said, "Good morning, Rashid. I want you to understand something. If you cooperate with us fully and give us information we can use, I will make sure you are taken to the United States and put into the witness protection program. And if your intelligence proves good, I might even get you work as a consultant for the intelligence services."

He gave his head rapid little shakes. "I will not help the West. You are Satan. You are the enemies of Allah, and Allah despises you!"

"I see. Well, Rashid, if you will not help us, all I can do is hand you over to Captain Gallin here, for her to take you back to Israel. I am pretty sure, after that, at least one of your friends will be willing to talk to us."

There were tears in his eyes. "I will not betray—"

Gallin cut him short. "We don't want you to betray anybody, Rashid." She gave a short laugh. "Hell, from what I am seeing, I think the one who got betrayed here is you. What did they tell you? Make a hit in Moscow, easy money, no reprisals, come back to Tehran to a hero's welcome? Is that what they told you?"

He didn't answer. I said, "You were set up, Rashid, you and your pals. I'm not interested in your connections back home or who you work for. I understand your spiritual loyalties, seriously I do." Gallin scowled at me with open contempt. I ignored her. "I am interested in one thing, Rashid. I'm interested in Russia. I want to know what Russia offered you."

Before he could answer, Gallin was at his throat again. "You won't talk to me, but ask yourself a question. Ask yourself this: Why were you prepared to go to Moscow and massacre fifteen innocent people—men, women, and children?" He swallowed, but she plowed on. "I'll tell you why, you son of a bitch, because they were not Muslims, and as far as you're concerned, if they are infidels, they are fair game; you can kill them, enslave them, and do what the hell you like with them. Isn't that right?"

"They are traitors to Allah." He said it, but he said it with not much conviction. I cut in.

"Save your justifications for when you meet your god, Rashid. If you were ready to massacre them while they were shopping, what's your problem with giving me information about them to save your life and the life of your friends? You think Putin believes in Allah? You think your god doesn't despise Putin? What does the Koran say? Nothing is more hateful in the eyes of Allah than an infidel? So talk to me. Informing on Putin is not betrayal of Allah. Especially if you are saving your comrades."

His eyes shifted from me to Gallin and back again. "My comrades? Save my friends?"

"You and your three friends go on witness protection."

"You will betray me. Like all infidels, you are a lying snake!"

Gallin leaned forward and slammed her hand on the

table top. It made him jump. She wasn't shouting yet, but she wasn't far off.

"No, Rashid. You don't get to murder innocent women and children and then accuse other people of being snakes! But the US won't betray you, and I'll tell you why! First because everybody in the States now wants to make every damn person in the world feel welcome and at home there, especially murdering bastards like you. It's called being inclusive. So once you're settled in there with a house and a car and a pool, you can get all your pals to go over and—"

"Gallin!"

She scowled at me a moment, then turned back to Rashid. "The other reason is because you can be useful to the CIA and the intelligence community in general. So they won't betray you as long as you don't betray them. The only people they betray these days are their allies."

I snapped at her, "You want to cut that out, Captain!"

She curled her lip. "You make me sick." She turned to George. "Both of you, groveling at their feet like frightened dogs!" She turned back to Rashid and pointed her finger at him like a gun. "You better pray to Allah that you don't get handed over to us, Rashid, because I promise you we won't be inclusive, and we won't put you in any witness protection program."

She stood and walked out, muttering over her shoulder, "Let me know when you're done groveling."

There was a moment's silence. Then I said, "I apologize. We are not here to prosecute you or attack you. We are here to ask for your cooperation."

"She is a Jew."

I felt the hot burn in my belly but suppressed it.

"Rashid, I am not looking for you to betray your religion or your spiritual leaders. I am asking you to give me information about the Russians. In your ideology, that is not betrayal."

He didn't say anything, but he was watching me, and his demeanor was different. I pressed him.

"Neither Sunni nor Shiite Muslims have ever held Russia as an enemy since the invasion of Afghanistan in the '80s. And now, more than ever, Russia and Islam have shared interests with Russia supporting Iran, Hamas, and Hezbollah in their jihad against Israel. So if that is the case, why would you choose now to perpetrate an atrocity in Moscow? It makes no sense at all."

Suddenly his lip curled and his nostrils dilated. He jerked his chin at me. "You're stupid," he said.

"Yeah? Maybe you're right. Enlighten me."

"You and your Jewish bitch, you're so bloody stupid. You know nothing!"

"I think we got that established, Rashid. Is there more, or is that it?"

"You think Russia paid us to make a massacre in Moscow? How bloody stupid would that be?"

"I am not looking to have a philosophical discussion with you, Rashid, about comparative stupidity. I am offering you protection and well-paid consulting work in exchange for information."

He leaned forward. "All right, I'll tell you who financed that job, the bloody British MI6!"

I was aware of George shifting in his chair.

"I may be stupid, like you said, Rashid, but I am not that

stupid. Why would MI6 want an Islamic attack on Moscow?"

"I don't know. Ask him." He jerked his head at George. "Your Western minds are so full of corruption and sickness, who knows why you do what you do?"

"So why'd you take the job? Why the hell would you work for the Brits? You hate them about as much as you hate us and the Israelis, don't you?"

He shrugged. "You are all loathsome in the eyes of Allah, but if the UK wants to provoke a war with Russia, I am happy to be the instrument for that war. What do I care what reasons the British government has? A war with Russia will break the Western economies as well as the Russian one, and the State of Islam will be able to rise, free from Satan's chains at last."

"Right. So how did MI6 go about this? You're sure it was MI6? How did they go about recruiting you for this job?"

"There was a message sent to the mullah in my village. Somebody recruiting for a very special operation."

"How did you find out it was MI6?"

"We were taken to a camp out in the desert in Iran. There we trained in the use of weapons and explosives, and after a month, a man came to visit us. He was a typical English upper class jerk. He wanted us to believe that this would be good for Islam, it would destabilize Russia and America and rob Israel of her biggest ally, and Britain was reshaping its future as an ally of the upcoming, oil-rich Islamic nations."

"And you believed him?"

"I believed the five million dollars he gave us."

"You believe Britain is realigning itself as a friend of Islam?"

"I don't know, and I don't care. Whether they like it or not, the UK will become an Islamic nation. It's already halfway there. The whole world will be Muslim one day, but if you ask me, the UK will be the first of the Western countries to subjugate itself to Allah."

"You might be right, Rashid. This guy give a name?"

"He said his name was Nepel."

"Nepel? What kind of name is that? Are you sure?"

"That's what he said. He was maybe six foot, fair, curly hair, blue eyes, and an upper class English accent."

I thought about it for a couple of minutes, and in the end I sighed and shook my head. "You know what I think, Rashid? I think you're full of crap, and I think I am going to hand you over to Captain Gallin so she can take you back to Israel with her."

His eyes went wide, and he started shaking his head. "No, what I am telling you is the truth, man! It's the truth!"

I turned to George. "Keep him isolated, will you? Don't let him talk to the other three. I'll talk to Tel Aviv this evening. Let me see Mohamed Hussein now, will you?"

Rashid was still shouting as they dragged him away to an isolation tent. He was saying he'd told me the truth.

THREE

GALLIN CAME IN AND DROPPED INTO HER CHAIR.

"That is some weird-ass story, Mason." I nodded. "It's hard enough to believe that any of the Islamic terror groups, either Sunni or Shiite, would have any interest at all in attacking Moscow. It is so unlikely as to be absurd, but that the Secret Intelligence Service should fund such an operation is laughable. Why would they? What possible interest could they have in doing that?"

"None."

"Right." And then, "Right?"

"Right."

"Who is it now?"

"Mohamed Hussein, the guy from Iraq."

"Oh, right. You wanna be bad cop this time? I want to engage with this guy. I like that triangle of fur on his face. Like three big moustaches."

"Okay. You CIA? I'm Mossad?"

Hussein was brought in five minutes later. He was sat

down and manacled to the table, as Rashid had been. George took up his seat where he had been before.

Gallin said, "You speak English, Mohamed?"

"I speak."

"Good. Because you need to understand the situation you are in. We have already spoken to Rashid. We are looking for cooperation, you understand? We do not want you to betray your religion or your faith; all we want is information. Okay?"

He blinked, but the three bars of hair remained immobile.

Gallin went on. "I want your cooperation. America wants your cooperation. The CIA wants to be a friend of the Islamic world, Mohamed. But if you don't help me, I cannot help you, and then my friend here, Captain Saul Heller, will take you from here to Tel Aviv. Saul is a captain in the IDF and a specialist in interrogation with the Mossad."

I leaned forward with my elbows on the table, and all three of his moustaches twitched. "I do not want to cooperate with you, Mohamed. I just want information." I smiled. It wasn't a nice smile. "Do you want to live forever, Mohamed? I can make you live forever. Come with me to Tel Aviv, and I promise you I can make every second of your life an eternity."

George sat up, and Gallin put a hand on my shoulder.

"Take it easy, Saul. Let's do this by the book, okay?"

I looked at her with ill-concealed contempt. "What book? I didn't notice no libraries on our way out here. Besides, if this guy chokes to death or accidentally loses an eye, I don't think anybody's gonna notice, Mary Sue."

George was on his feet, looking mad. "I am going to have to ask you—"

I cut him short. "Yeah, okay, keep your panties on, Jeeves. I'll keep my goddamn mouth shut." I turned to Mohamed with an ugly leer. "All I am asking, Mohamed, is you don't tell her nothin'. Let's you and me talk, man to man, back in Israel."

"Enough!" Gallin was scowling. "If you are going to be part of this interrogation, Captain Heller, I am going to have to ask you to restrain yourself!"

I muttered something ugly, and she turned to Mohamed, whose eyes were bright with fear.

"Please, miss, don't make me go with the Jew. I tell you everything you want to know." His head had started flopping from side to side. "I am good family man. I have two wife, eight children. I need my eyes for work. Please. My family need me. I cooperate. I tell you everything you are needing to know."

"Who recruited you, Mohamed?"

"It was message in my mosque. Imam tell us, all young men, they are looking for God's warriors, for a jihad. It pays good. Who will go? I say I will go."

I snarled. "In spite of your two wives and your eight children?"

"It pays good money. They say there is no danger. I go."

"So you told the imam you'd do the job. What happened next?"

"They take us to Iran, to a camp in the desert, and there they are training us with guns."

"How long were you there?"

"Maybe one month."

"Did you meet the man who recruited you?"

"Yes, he comes to the camp. He give the chief of the training camp many millions of dollars. He tell us what we must do."

"Who was he? Did he tell you his name? Where he was from?"

He nodded. "He is English man, from secret police. He is blond, tall, blue eyes, and his name is Nepel. He is interesting man, like an angel. He say that he come to bring war between the East and the West, so that the old way will fall, the false gods will die, and Islam, the way of the true god, will rule all the Earth, allahu akbar!"

I said, "He was English, blond, blue eyes, and he said that?"

"He was like an angel from God. He said many things. He said that soon the Kingdom of England would fall, and Islam would rule there. But we must help by bringing war to these countries."

Gallin cut in, "So, Mohamed, how did you get your weapons into Russia? I mean, you had assault rifles, pistols..."

"No problem. We drive into Russia by car, no problem, and in Moscow, a man meet us and give us car. In the trunk of car is all the weapons. We shoot everybody and 'nother, different car is waiting, and we escape to Iran. This is our instructions. But in Iran, police is arrest us. I don't know why. They send us back to Moscow. But you..." He gestured at us though he didn't finish the sentence.

Gallin seized on it. "We saved your lives."

"Yes." He hesitated. "You are MI6? This is why you save us?"

I saw her glance over at George, who was frowning. Eventually, she said, "We are friends with MI6, and we are not going to let Moscow or Tehran take you or hurt you. You have been tricked very badly, and we want to help you. Can you tell me anything else that might help us?"

He nodded. "We go to London."

"You went to *London?* What for?"

He slowly hunched his shoulders, arched his eyebrows, and spread his hands. What you could see of his expression under his three moustaches was plaintive.

"I don't know. I say to Omar, 'Why we are here, Omar?' He say me, 'I don't know, Mohamed. God will guide us. Allahu akbar!'"

"All four of you went?"

"Yes. We meet Sunny also. He is also from MI6."

"He told you that?"

"Yes." He tilted his head on one side and spread his hands in that plaintive gesture again. "He is talking most to Rashid, because Rashid is like English. He talk good English. He tells, 'When you have kill everyone, you communicate with me and tell me. We teach you how to use social media for communicate. We train you here in London.' But we already know how do this. We know what they training us."

I said, "So let me see if I understand this. They had you go over to the UK to train you in using social media to communicate with them, but the trip and the training were completely unnecessary."

He nodded once using his whole body for emphasis and grinned. "Yes."

Gallin turned to George. "I think we're done here for

now. Let me talk to Omar and then Hassan. Then I want to talk to you."

He arched an eyebrow at her, but he didn't say anything.

Over the next couple of hours, we talked to Omar bin Abbas from France and Syria and then Hassan from Afghanistan. Their English was halting and far from fluent, but in essence, they told the same story as Mohamed. They had been trained in firearms in Iran, they had met an angelic English Muslim with blond hair and blue eyes, and then they had been taken to London for completely unnecessary training in using social media as a means of communication. When we were done with them, I told George I wanted to talk to Rashid again, alone.

When he'd gone, Gallin said, "What's the idea?"

"He's the only one who knows why they went to London."

"How the hell do you know that?"

"Because he's the only one who didn't tell us they had been there. I'm going to tell him you're making arrangements for the flight to Tel Aviv and he has twenty minutes before you get back to set the record straight."

She nodded. "Okay. After that, I want to put the screws on George. There is something wrong here that's wrong and ain't right."

"I agree."

She got up and left, and a couple of minutes later, Rashid was brought in and manacled to the table again. The soldiers left, and George went to take his seat.

"George, you want to give us five minutes? I'm trying to save Rashid's life here." He hesitated. I gave him an almost invisible nod and added, "Everybody will thank you, especially Rashid."

"Five minutes."

"That's all I need."

He left, and I turned to Rashid. "Captain Gallin has gone to make arrangements for you to be flown to Tel Aviv." He turned a sickly yellow color. I said, "Don't talk. Just listen. The Israelis are an efficient, effective, highly skilled fighting force, and they do not crack under pressure. They just become more efficient, effective, and skilled. They have centuries of experience facing existential threats, and it has become a part of how they approach life. Now your little expedition to Moscow, once it plays out, will not only threaten to bring down the Western alliance and its economy, it will, as collateral damage, present Israel with the greatest threat to its existence since the rise of the Third Reich. So I am going to ask you a question, Rashid. If you were an officer with the Mossad, locked in a soundproof room with Rashid Patel, where would you draw the line in interrogating him?"

I raised a hand. "I know, torture elicits unreliable intelligence. But look at this: In one morning's work, just by separating you guys, I found out that you were all taken to London to meet Sunny, who spoke more to you than to anybody else, about using social media for communication.

"Now, imagine, if I take you to a soundproof room, and every bit of intelligence I draw out of you, I triple-check, not only through my London field office, but against your three pals, and I punish you, mercilessly, without humanity or pity, every time you lie to me. How long do you think you're going to hold out?"

I checked my watch. "She'll be back in fifteen minutes to take you to the airfield."

His face was rigid and sickly. He kept swallowing, and his pupils were tiny pinpricks. When he spoke, it was like the Hulk had a grip on his throat.

"I don't want to go to Tel Aviv. Please don't let her take me."

I leaned forward. "Pal, I don't give a good goddamn if you go to Tel Aviv or to hell where you belong. So I'll tell you this: You tell me about London and what the purpose of that visit was, or you leave here in a quarter of an hour and you will *never* see the light of day again."

"Okay, I'll talk. But please, don't let her take me."

I spoke, punctuating the sentence with my finger stabbing the table.

"I want every-single-goddamn-detail! I want to know what color shorts Sunny was wearing! I want to know if somebody coughed or blew his nose! *I want every-goddamned-detail!* Cross me, try to play me, try to get smart, and I swear, Rashid, by tonight you will be begging to be put out of your misery. If you lie to me, we *will* find out, and you *will* pay."

"I am willing to cooperate."

I leaned back in my chair. "That's a wise choice, Rashid, but I have to tell you, first thing this morning I was offering you witness protection and consultancy work with the intelligence community. That is off the table now. You want it back on the table, you are going to have to work for it and convince me you are for real. Understood?"

He nodded. I said, "Good. So tell me about London,

and remember, we will be triple-checking everything you tell us."

He sighed, and I saw tears in his eyes.

"After the training camp, Nepel said he wanted us to go to London before traveling to Moscow. I asked him why. I didn't think there was any need for that. He said he wanted to introduce us to an officer in MI6 who was running the operation."

"What was his name?"

"Sunny. Least, that's what he called himself. Pretty sure it wasn't his real name. So we met Sunny at a house in Willesden. I think he was Iranian, born in London, and he told us he wanted us to stay there for ten days and do a training course on how to use social media to communicate covert messages. It was stupid, typical arrogance, like we wouldn't know how to do that. I'll tell you something else: If that is their level, we could teach *them* a thing or two."

"Where was this house? I want the address."

"It was 194 B, Walm Lane, in Willesden."

"So they weren't real professional, huh?"

"Not at all. They were like amateurs."

"What other kind of stupid things did they do? Did they do like class photos, film you, record you..."

He stared at me for a long moment. In the end, I sighed and gave a small laugh. "You just answered me, right, Rashid? If they hadn't, you would have dismissed the question as stupid. But you didn't. You stared at me and refused to answer. So they did. They took photos—and film? Please remember you still have a seat booked on the next flight to Tel Aviv. So tell me about it."

He swore softly and rubbed his face with his hands.

"They filmed every damned class that we did. I was furious, and I had a couple of flaming rows with Nepel and especially with Sunny. I told him it was an unnecessary risk. I told him the whole operation was unprofessional. There was no 'need to know' protocol, no compartmentalization. It was bloody amateur."

"Did that make you suspicious?"

"It should have, but I just thought it was the typical arrogance and stupidity of the British."

I gave a small snort. "You hate the British because of the Empire, right?"

"Amongst other things."

"Right, but you don't create the greatest empire in history by being stupid, Rashid. It never crossed your mind that you were being set up?"

He shook his head.

"You never stopped to question why MI6 would want to false flag an attack by jihadists against Moscow?"

"Yes, of course! But what my imam told me at the mosque was that they were trying to break the alliance between Moscow and Tehran."

"And that didn't worry you? Hamas, Hezbollah, and Iran need Moscow's support."

"Of course, but in the first place, Russia is not Muslim, so God will be happy with an attack on them by us, and in the second place, when the attack happens, we immediately tell Moscow it was not us. It was MI6, and we can prove it."

He went suddenly quiet.

"You can prove it?"

He sighed again. "We kept evidence from the beginning. We took photos and films of our own. And we were careful always to hide our faces, even in the pictures and footage they took. So we could always deny it was us, but we could prove it was MI6."

"What happened to the footage and the pictures they took?"

"I don't know. Sunny had them."

"Where is all the evidence you collected?"

"I hid it where nobody would ever think to look for it."

"Where?"

"In London."

"Where, Rashid?"

He shook his head. "If I tell you, I am dead meat. I'll give you the exact location when you give me a guarantee I'll be put in witness protection and the Mossad will not be informed of where I am." A sickly leer twisted his face. "Or would you rather I told the Israelis where it is?"

George poked his head into the tent.

"You done?"

"Yeah, we're done." To Rashid I said, "I am undecided. You have a good think about whether you want me as an ally or as an enemy. We'll talk again in the morning."

George took him away, and I sat thinking for a while, staring at the empty chair. Then I reached for my cell and called Gallin.

FOUR

We were in Roger's tent. He had supplied us with strong coffee in tin mugs, and we were seated around his table.

"One thing strikes me forcefully above all the others," I told them. "And that is that they all tell the same story. That in itself could be the product of training and rehearsal, but two factors argue against that." I held up one finger. "One, they stand to gain nothing from the story they have concocted. In fact, it guarantees them as everybody's enemy. And two"—I held up two fingers—"Rashid did not want the most important part of this story to come out. It was only when he realized the others had talked that he admitted it."

George asked, "What part are you referring to?"

"The fact that they were taken to an address in London, ostensibly to teach them how to use social media for communication. He says his two contacts, Nepel and Sunny, were incompetent. They didn't seem to understand the concept of need to know or compartmentalization. He also says lots of films and photographs were taken."

"By his supposed MI6 handlers?"

I nodded. "Yeah, but he says he and Mohamed, Omar, and Hassan started taking photographs and videos of their own and amassing evidence."

George frowned. "Evidence of what?"

"Evidence to prove two things: A, that the operation was set up and paid for by MI6 for the purpose of breaking Moscow's relationship with Tehran; and B, that though they have the evidence, they were not participants."

"Where is that evidence now?"

I gave a humorless laugh. "That's what I asked him. He said it was in London, where nobody would expect it to be hidden, and that he would tell me in exchange for a guarantee that he would go into the witness protection program and that the Mossad would never find out where he was."

His gaze shifted to the brilliant gash of sunlight at the entrance to his tent. After a moment, he drew breath and shook his head. There was a helplessness to the gesture.

"Somewhere no one would suspect in a city of over five hundred square miles and a population of nine million people. The variables are practically infinite." He looked at me. "What about the other three? Would they know?"

Gallin said, "I spoke to them. They all said Rashid had hidden it. They didn't know where. He's not as stupid as he looks. We'll have to make the deal."

I nodded. "No question about it, but let him sweat till morning. I'll tell him before breakfast the Pentagon has instructed me that the only way he stays out of the Mossad's hands is if he tells me where the evidence is. Otherwise there is no deal."

Gallin made the face of doubtfulness. "He won't go for it. The moment he gives us that information, he loses his shield. He won't do that unless he gets something in return he can take to the bank."

"I know." I shrugged. "But people in fear, under stress, make stupid mistakes. We have nothing to lose by waiting till morning. If he doesn't crack, we give him the deal, and we take all four of them back to DC." I glanced at George. "Agreed?"

He nodded. "Agreed." And after a moment, he added, "I don't know who the hell is responsible for this, but I can assure you it was not us. The incompetence..." He trailed off, narrowing his eyes first at Gallin and then at me. "The incompetence reeks of the Russians. But that doesn't make any sense at all."

I nodded and glanced at Gallin. She watched George for a while, and I wondered if she was going to tell him about Nero's thoughts on the subject. Instead she said, "None of it makes any sense. Let's see what we can get out of these guys when we get them back to DC."

We thanked him for the coffee and made our way back to our own tent. There I called Nero on the secure ODIN line.

"Report."

"This is an unholy mess."

"That much we knew, Alex. Can you please be more precise?"

I outlined the facts for him. "And like George said, none of it makes much sense, unless there is a really convoluted plot to cause a crisis in NATO itself."

He grunted. "One or two years ago, nobody would have believed that the United States would betray Israel as an ally. But when a particular war threatens the economic interests of your ally, that ally will almost certainly betray you. Britain, I am afraid, is in a very vulnerable position at the moment. If her allies back away from a conflict with Russia, she will be in serious trouble."

"Okay, I hear you, sir. We'll send them back to DC under armed guard in the morning. Meanwhile, I think Gallin and I should go to London to find the evidence Rashid says he left there. If that means offering him a deal, I think we should do that. The stakes are too high to be messing around."

"I agree. Use your discretion, and I shall back you up."

We had some dinner, and by ten o'clock, we were in our cots, drifting off to sleep.

The first shouts came at four in the morning. Urgent, raising the alarm. I was out of bed and reaching for my weapon before I was awake. Gallin collided with me in the dark. "What the hell!"

"Get dressed!" I snarled and was out through the tent opening while she pulled on her shirt. I found soldiers milling, and among them George making for our tent.

"The prisoners," he said.

"What about them? What's going on?"

"They're dead."

"*What?*"

Gallin emerged from the tent behind me, echoing the same question.

George was talking fast. "The sentries do a routine check on them every half hour. Did—on the last check, less than a minute ago, when Sergeant McTavish looked in on Rashid..."

He trailed off and closed his eyes. I pushed past him, shouting, "Sergeant McTavish! Where is Sergeant McTavish?"

A growl through the trees said, "I'm right here! Will everybody stop shouting!"

I followed the sound and found him hunkered down beside Hassan's body, playing a flashlight over the corpse. He glanced up at me and pointed at Hassan's throat, where there was a small, scorched black hole.

"Point blank range. Twenty-two mil. I'd say suppressed and subsonic. My guess is it shattered his vertebrae, paralyzing him, but didn't exit. A silent kill by a feller who knew what he was doing."

"That description fits everyone in this camp. Anyone could have done it."

He studied my face a moment. His lack of expression was menacing. When he spoke, his voice could have brought snow to the Sahara.

"Everyone here has the skills, aye, but not everyone is capable of doing it, Mr. Mason. I'll stand by every blade in the camp. So if it was an inside job, you can narrow your search to Captain Gallin, George Locke, and yer good self."

He allowed his gaze to linger a second, just to make sure I got the insolence, then said, "Here, gimme a hand, will ya?"

We rolled the body on its face so the back of his neck was exposed. Then he pulled a Fairbairn and Sykes fighting knife from his boot and slid it gently across the area where the man's neck met his skull. No blood emerged, but he pulled back the edges of the two-inch wound and told me, "Here, hold it open."

I leaned closer and pulled back the edges of the cut. He introduced the point of his knife and began to tease at the tissue. I could see bits of shattered bone, and then bit by bit, he managed to extract a small, distorted lump of lead. He held it up for me to see.

"If we're very lucky, there might be a casing about. My guess is he would use a revolver to avoid that. If he was planning to kill all four of 'em, as he obviously was, time would be an important factor, and he would not want to be scrabbling in the dirt for his casings. But you never know"—he leered—"maybe Santa Claus exists after all."

A bright light bathed the inside of the tent from the entrance flap. It was Gallin.

"He would have stood about here," she said and reached out her arm to where Hassan would have been. "Bam! And the shell would have fallen..." She shone the flashlight at my feet. "Stand up and step back a bit."

I did as she said and saw the glint of brass. McTavish reached in his tunic and pulled out a pencil. He slipped the pencil inside the casing and lifted it, muttering, "Well, I'll be damned..." He shone his flashlight on it, then held it up for us to look at. "Don't touch it. This professional assassin is so feckin' incompetent he might well have left prints. Barnaul," he added. "It's a Russian round."

George's voice came from behind Gallin, instructing someone to go get some plastic sandwich bags. Then he said, "Mr. Mason, I'll need you to take those and have them analyzed, and have the results and your report on this incident forwarded to the Secret Intelligence Service."

He glanced at Gallin. "That goes for you also, Captain Gallin."

She nodded. "Sure."

I said, "That's why we're here."

"You are witness to this event and this exchange, Sergeant McTavish."

"I am, Mr. Locke."

"Will you show Captain Gallin and Mr. Mason the other bodies, please. See if this incompetent ass has left any more shells behind, or any other evidence." There was a movement behind him, and he handed Gallin a bunch of plastic bags. "Just in case we get lucky."

Each of the four men had been killed in the same way. Each had scorch marks on his throat, and in each case, we recovered a shell casing a few feet from the body. As Gallin knelt to collect the last of these, McTavish said, "He just didn't give a damn. This is not incompetence. It's more like 'screw you.' He just didn't give a damn if the casing was found or no."

Gallin looked at him and nodded.

We made our way across the clearing to Captain Eddy 'Spud' Walker's tent. There he was talking to George over a mug of coffee. He poured us some as we approached. I accepted one, glanced from George to the captain, and said, "I'm not sure who I'm talking to, but this evidence and the bodies needs to be shipped to Andrews Air Force Base, Maryland, care of the Office of the Director of Intelligence Networks. I need you to do that this morning. And I need you to get us to Warsaw for breakfast. Can you do that?"

Captain Eddy 'Spud' Walker nodded. "I'll call in a chopper. What happened here?"

"On the face of it, a Russian assassin got into your camp and assassinated these four men, one after another, and was quite happy to leave his Russian-made shells behind. Then he slipped like a ghost into the night."

The captain said, "That doesn't make a lot of sense. If they know our location, why didn't they simply send a drone or a rocket and wipe us all out? Why the difficulty and the risk involved in sending in a man, who could easily have been caught?"

"That is a really good question, Spud. And all I can think of is that they wanted the four terrorists dead, but they didn't want the rest of you dead. What they wanted was for you, or us, to find those Russian casings."

He narrowed his eyes and glanced at George. "That makes even less sense. Why on Earth would they want to spare SAS soldiers operating in the area and advertise the fact that they were here?"

Gallin said, "Because an all-out strike is what the Russians would do. And the Russians are the supposed victims here, remember? As far as they are concerned, MI6 are the aggressors. Either way, if you want my opinion, I'd get my boys out of here fast, just in case they change their minds."

"Yes, we're striking camp as we speak. But I must say, your reasoning is a little cryptic."

"Yeah." She nodded. "So is theirs."

"Either way," he said with a grunt, "nobody will be happier than the Ukrainians if we do get drawn in. They'll be praying NATO gets dragged in on our coattails."

"That," I said, "is something we all need to be praying for."

Half an hour later, we were speeding low over the vast, sweeping plains of what had once been the bread basket of the Soviet Union in a Sikorsky S-61R, headed west toward Poland and Warsaw. It was a seven hundred mile flight, but pushing the bird to its maximum of one hundred and sixty-five miles per hour, we figured we could make it to Warsaw's Baza Lotnictwa military airbase by ten a.m. and have coffee and scrambled eggs while the ODIN Gulfstream was refueling to take us to London.

We didn't talk much, but Gallin said, "Why deliberately leave Russian casings, Mason? It doesn't make sense. If they are trying to frame the Brits, why didn't they use British ammo casings? I mean, if it was a stupid mistake, I could buy it. The Russians aren't exactly Ninja Central, but this was clearly deliberate."

"Yeah." I gazed out at the plains and occasional woodlands speeding past below. "I'll tell you something else," I said. "Those guys, Rashid, Omar, Mohammed, and Hassan, they didn't fight back; they weren't even alarmed. From the position each one of them was in, they stood up and were not expecting to be shot."

"Yeah, I noticed that. They knew whoever it was. Did they think they were being rescued?"

We stared at each other a while. Finally I gave my head a small shake. "I don't know, but it's like I'm waiting for something to come out of left field, and I don't even know where left field is."

She was quiet a while longer, then: "I think left field might be 194 B Walm Lane, in Willesden."

"Yeah, you could be right. Or anywhere else in London."

"We need to find Sunny." I looked at her and nodded.

She went on. "Whatever game the SIS may be playing, I can't believe ODIN didn't know these guys had arrived in London. They must have kept tabs on them. We need to talk to Sir Lacklan Orme."

"You're right. It's weird. But he would have mentioned—"

She cut me short, shaking her head. "Mason, we only found out half this stuff a few hours ago. ODIN London might have been watching these guys routinely without making the connection."

I pulled my cell from my pocket and dialed. A woman's voice came on. She might have been directing you where to sit at a Women's Institute meeting.

"Good morning. Could I please ask you to state your name and the purpose of your call after the beep? Thank you!"

"Alex Mason, wanting to speak to Sir Lacklan Orme."

It took a couple of seconds for voice recognition to identify me, then Sir Lacklan's voice came on the line.

"Alex, how good to hear from you. Are you aware of the time?"

"Yes, sir. We are about to catch a flight to London; we should touch down about twelve noon. We need to talk to you on a matter of the utmost urgency. Can you meet us at City Airport?"

"Well, um..."

"I'm afraid I have to insist, Sir Lacklan. The futures of NATO and the United Kingdom are in the balance. Sir, the future of the West is at stake."

FIVE

It was half past noon as we climbed into the back of Sir Lacklan Orme's Rolls Royce. He regarded us in turn as we settled with a smile that had been aborted by a wince.

"Is this the American propensity to overstate things, Alex? The future of the West at stake?"

I narrowed my eyes at him and said, "Six hundred British soldiers of the Gloucestershire Regiment were being hammered by vastly superior Chinese forces at the Imjin River in Korea. Brigadier Tom Brodie radioed the American General Robert Soule at Joint Command that things were 'a bit sticky.' The American general understood this to mean that the Brits were coping, when what he meant was that they were being slaughtered from every side. As it was, they held out for four days against a total of thirty thousand Chinese soldiers, killing ten thousand of them. Fifty-nine of their own men were killed, thirty-nine escaped, but five hundred were captured and spent years in

Chinese prison camps. They are credited with having saved Seoul, but that British understatement cost a lot of lives. If Brigadier Brodie had said, 'General, for Christ's sake, we are being massacred here!' things would have gone differently."

We were pulling out onto the North Woolwich Road, headed west toward the city center. Sir Lacklan regarded me with no expression for a moment, then smiled suddenly.

"Point taken. Perhaps you would care to explain to me why you believe Western civilization is on the brink of collapse."

Gallin cut in and outlined the situation, then added, "Those men were brought to London by two Englishmen. They were put up at a house on Walm Lane in Willesden, and they were given training. All of this was filmed and photographed. Which on the face of it seems like an act of complete stupidity and incompetence."

He blinked. "On the face of it..."

"Yesterday we had secured an agreement from the leader of these four terrorists that he would give us a full account of what happened, how they were recruited, who they spoke to —they had taken footage and photographs themselves. And in the morning Rashid was going to give us the exact location where they had stashed their evidence."

"But...?"

I said, "They were murdered during the night. A single shot to the throat with a suppressed .22. The shell casings were left behind and proved to be from Russian Barnaul bullets."

His brow clenched. "But that doesn't... Why would they...?"

We were speeding along the A13 toward Whitechapel. Gallin broke in on his pauses.

"There is a fundamental contradiction in their actions. Either be upfront and say, 'Okay, we are Russians and we are going to wipe out this British camp, which shouldn't be here in the first place,' or secretly kill the prisoners but use British ammo casings. Either way leaves open the question of why they wanted those prisoners dead, but that contradiction stands. Why the secrecy if you are going to leave Russian shell casings behind? And why not attack the site as a whole with drones?"

"Yes." He said it absently as we passed St Paul's Cathedral, headed toward the Temple. "There is nothing to be gained by advertising the fact that the men were killed by Russians."

"Unless," I said, "we look at it from the other angle. If the casings had been British, or even absent altogether, suspicion would have fallen on the men in the camp. But if Russian Barnaul ammo was used, it points to a Russian hit and shifts suspicion away from the men at the camp."

There was resentment in his eyes, and he didn't talk again until we had dismounted from the car at Whitehall Court and ascended to his office. Once he had settled himself behind his desk, he said, "I cannot accept that a serving member of the SAS would betray his country. It is out of the question."

Gallin surprised me by saying, "We don't suspect Captain Spud Walker or any of his men, sir. But I would reserve my judgment on George Locke."

"George is a good man. He's been with the Intelligence Service for over ten years."

I said, "It's a process of elimination, sir. Eliminate the impossible and what you are left with must be the truth. We can be ninety-nine percent certain that the SAS men out there were loyal. Neither Captain Gallin nor I stand to gain anything at all from murdering those men. That leaves either an actual assassin deployed by the Russians, who broke into the camp and murdered four men—"

Gallin interjected, "Which beggars belief. First of all, to break into an SAS camp in a conflict area without being detected is all but impossible, but if you are that good that you manage it, and you are then so stupid as to leave shell casings behind that show you are Russian?" She shook her head. "No."

I went on. "So it is at least possible that there was a Russian operative already in the camp. For my money, it is more than possible; it is probable."

He scowled at me. "You are suggesting that George Locke is a Russian agent."

"I'm saying we need to be alert to the possibility. And there is another thing. When these four guys arrived in London, you or MI5 must have noticed them. They must have been on your radar, even if it didn't register who they were at the time. "

Gallin had been messing with her phone. Now she said, "I've sent you their mug shots and their names. And we need this to move. There is photographic and video evidence taken by these Sunny and Nepel guys, and there is the stuff recorded by Rashid. We need to get our hands on that evidence because if that evidence gets back to Moscow, the UK is going to have the mother of all shitstorms on its hands."

He sighed very deeply and scanned the photographs. Eventually he nodded.

"All right, I am going to arrange a couple of meetings. You go and get some rest. I'll be in touch later today."

WE GOT BACK to Gallin's place off Holland Park Avenue about half an hour later, and while she threw a couple of frozen pizzas in the oven, I cracked a couple of beers, and we collapsed in her living room. I stretched out on the sofa, drained half my beer, and closed my eyes while she sank into a large calico armchair and put her feet up on what we call an ottoman and the Brits call a pouf.

After a moment, I heard the TV come on, and that weird rhythm of speech which, in all the languages of the world, means you're listening to the news. I didn't pay much attention until I heard Gallin get up and go into the kitchen. Then I heard the creak of the oven door opening and the hum of the fan oven. The door slammed and plates rattled. The smell of hot pepperoni reached my nostrils and made them happy. Then the TV said, "President Vladimir Putin has accused Britain of perpetrating an act of war against the Russian Federation, and he has stated in a press conference at the Kremlin broadcast live on Russian Television that has caused deep concern across Western governments, that there will be reprisals, and the United Kingdom will deeply regret its temerity and its arrogance."

I had sat up and Gallin was standing in the kitchen doorway holding two plates of pizza. She was staring at the TV. The anchor was asking what the supposed acts of war were, and they cut back to a woman standing in Red Square, holding a red microphone.

"Breaking news: The Kremlin asserts that the recent terrorist attack in Moscow's TSUM shopping mall, opposite the Bolshoi Theatre, was in fact funded, planned, and orchestrated by Britain's MI6. This in itself was an act of war, they say, but they also claim that, having had the perpetrators arrested in Tehran, the British SAS, acting deep within Russian sovereign territory, carried out a raid on a convoy carrying the terrorists to Moscow for interrogation and trial. They claim the SAS group killed ten Russian security guards and took the terrorists away with them."

Back in the studio, the newscaster at the desk asked, "What is the feeling, Joanna, among your contacts? Are the Kremlin's allegations true? Are they even likely?"

"Well, Karen, it is true that the SAS are known for pulling off daredevil operations that to anyone else would seem harebrained and reckless. On the other hand, MI6 paying Muslim terrorists to strike at a Moscow shopping mall does seem pretty farfetched. Though Konstantin Chuychenko, the Russian Minister of Justice, has stated that Russia will be adducing evidence to the International Court of Justice and calling for the British government and the Prime Minister to be tried for war crimes."

They cut back to the studio. "So far we have heard nothing regarding how other states have responded to this accusation, but we will keep you updated as and when new information comes in. But now we'll go to Terry McCahan at Downing Street. Terry, has there been a statement from the Prime Minister yet regarding these accusations?"

Gallin muttered, "Oy vey" under her breath and came

and sat down. Terry was squinting at the camera and pressing his ear.

"Karen, good afternoon. There has been a press release, which I shall read to you in a moment, but what we have heard since Vladimir Putin made these allegations is that there has been a veritable flurry of activity, with the ministers for Defence, the Home Office, the Foreign Office and the heads of MI5—*and* the SIS—all being summoned to Downing Street for meetings with the Prime Minister. I am told he will be making a public statement later this afternoon, but so far, everybody is keeping very quiet, and the only official response has been this press release from Number Ten."

He held it up and read from it. "'The Prime Minister of Great Britain states categorically that at no time has he personally, or through the Cabinet, or any member of His Majesty's Government acting in any official capacity, sought, instigated, approved, engineered or facilitated, or in any other way attempted to encourage or bring about any kind of terrorist attack on Russian soil or anywhere else. The Russian president's allegations are rejected in their entirety and in the strongest possible terms.' That, Karen, is all we have so far, but I understand that the Russian Ambassador has been summoned, and aids of the Prime Minister and the Foreign Secretary are feverishly telephoning foreign leaders, and the PM himself is said to have spoken privately to both President Biden *and* Donald Trump."

She looked at me, and for the first time since I had met her, I saw fear in her eyes.

"It's started. This is completely outside our experience. Nobody has lived through anything like this, Mason, not since Germany invaded Poland. Only this is even bigger and more dangerous."

I said, "It's saber rattling."

"It's not saber rattling, Mason. He is provoking a war with Britain, and he believes Europe and the US will back away from the confrontation."

I shook my head. "We can't think that way, Gallin. It's too big. We focus on the next step."

She nodded. "Yeah." She stared at the screen, then looked back at me. "Sunny."

"Sunny and Rashid's evidence."

"Right."

Her phone rang and jangled, and we both jumped. She picked it up and listened for a moment. Then she said, "Yeah, we saw it."

She put it on speaker and leaned back in her chair. It was Gabriel, her father, the head of the Mossad's London field office. He was saying, "Sir Lacklan has asked me to meet with him this evening."

"What for?"

"What for? What do you think? If Russia, God forbid, if Russia declared war on the UK five, ten years ago, the whole Western World would have rallied to support her. Now? Today? It's a very different setup. England used to be the cornerstone that held the United States, the European Union, the Commonwealth, and Israel together. It was the middle man. Now it is the weak link in a rotten chain. Break England, and each will go his own way, Europe, Australasia, the United States—and England and Israel will be left to be eaten by the wolves."

Gallin looked at me across the room. She puffed out her

cheeks and blew. "Did Sir Lacklan tell you about the men we are interested in?"

"He said if I called you you'd tell me. This is how it is— are you there, Alex?"

"I'm here."

"This is how it is; I need to have the head of a foreign, international espionage agency tell me to call my own daughter before she talks to me. What do you think about that?"

Thankfully he laughed before I could answer him. Gallin was busy with her phone. She said, "You got them? I just sent them."

"I got them. I already had them. I told Sir Lacklan to go screw himself and made him send me the pictures. They are the people we were watching. We exchanged intelligence with MI5 and the Office of Intelligence Networks. But back then, when we were watching them, nobody knew who they were. We were aware of them, curious, but we couldn't connect them with anything. Because they were an unattached group of single men, obviously Muslims, we watched them, and we kept MI5 in the loop. But it slipped by SIS and ODIN."

I said, "What do you know about them?"

"They were camping out at a house in Willesden, 194 B Walm Lane. They had three visitors. Two of them came just twice. One of them we have absolutely no idea who he is. He is tall, fair, well dressed. We got a few shots of him, but he is very hard to identify. The other we tracked down and found he was an actor doing gigs for money. You know the sort of thing. He will play a policeman in a practical joke, arrest your husband or wife at the altar when you are getting married, pretend to actually get murdered in a murder mystery party. We asked CID to ask him what he was doing at Walm Lane. He said he was pretending to be an instructor in social media for four Muslim guys."

"Jesus Christ!" I said out loud. "That's all we damn well needed! An actor!"

"It's not that much of a surprise, Mason." It was Gallin. "They said it was crap and they didn't learn anything they didn't know already."

"Now we know why. I'm figuring Mr. Smooth was Nepel. So what about the third guy? The one who came more often?"

"I think he is the one you called Sunny. We kept tabs on him and found out where he lived."

Gallin sat up. "Great. Where is he? Let's go get him!"

"No. It's not that easy. He disappeared about five days ago. He has a wife—or a girlfriend, you never know these days. It might be a transgender boyfriend. Who knows? But she is still at the house. Maybe she can tell you something. I am sending you the address with the photos we have."

I said, "We'll go talk to her. Do you have the place bugged? Or her phone tapped? It would be interesting to listen to her conversations after we talk to her."

He was quiet for a moment, then grunted. "You might think, Alex, that if we were a ruthless, highly skilled organization fighting for survival in an increasingly insane, hostile world, we would have her house bugged and her phone tapped. But clearly, that would be illegal. So we would not do it." You could almost hear him shrug. "Unless some official from the Mossad accidentally stumbled in there while drunk and mistakenly let some bugs drop, and some wire taps got connected in some crazy, freak accident. But how likely is that? Million to one chance."

"That's a relief. I thought you might be breaking the law. What about the house in Walm Lane? Do you know what happened there?"

"We've been keeping tabs on it also, in case somebody came back. At the moment, it is empty."

My phone started ringing. I said, "It's Sir Lacklan."

Gabriel said, "I'll probably see you this evening."

He hung up, and I answered. "Sir Lacklan."

"You've seen the news?"

"Yes."

"I am hosting an extremely urgent meeting this evening at eight in my office. I should like you to be there, please."

"We'll be there, Sir Lacklan. We'll be there for sure. But we have a couple of things we need to do before that."

"Very well."

"Sir, are you listening to Sunny's house?"

"That would be illegal."

"Yeah, I know, but are you doing it?"

"Yes."

"Good. We might get something tonight."

SIX

WE GOT TO WALM LANE ABOUT SIX P.M. IT WAS A leafy road with large, detached late Victorian redbricks. Out front, they had crescent moon driveways framed by rose-bushes and London plane trees. Out back, they had long lawns framed by towering sycamores, beach and ash, that provided a lot of privacy.

Gallin parked her twenty-year-old S-Type Jaguar in the driveway, obscuring the view of the door from the street. She climbed out, hunkered down by the lock, and spent about fifteen seconds applying a set of skills she had not learned at private school. The latch clicked, and the door swung open.

We slipped inside, and I closed the door behind us.

It was very still and quiet. Gallin wrinkled her nose. She said quietly, "Aftershave. Expensive but..." She made a face of disgust and put her fingers together like an Italian chef.

I said, "Cloying." She nodded. I went on, "You want to take the kitchen and I'll take living room and dining room?"

She nodded and moved down the hall with her new

BUL SAS Tac held out in front of her. I pulled my Sig P226 and toed open the door to the dining room. It was open plan, from the big bow window with views of the drive, Gallin's Jag and Walm Lane, all the way to the broad French windows that overlooked the lawn and the backyard. In front of me, there was a long table with six chairs and a colorful bowl of bananas that were going black. The floor was bare boards. Beyond the table, there was a bookcase, but all the books were on the wooden floor.

I crossed the boards to the living area. There was an old, sage green sofa, two matching armchairs, a long coffee table that was probably fashionable when the Beatles had pudding-bowl haircuts, and a large, flat screen TV on a stand on the floor. The sofa and the chairs had been tipped over, their cushions eviscerated, and the backs and underside slashed and torn open.

A door in the wall a little beyond where the sofa should have been opened, and Gallin entered, paused, and took in the room. She moved to one side and jerked her head at the kitchen. Everything that should have been in a drawer or a cupboard was on the floor.

"I guess somebody had the same idea as us, huh?"

She offered me a humorless smile. "You think?"

I gave my head a twitch. "Either that or they have real big mice." I moved back toward the hall. "Let's have a look upstairs."

I climbed the steps with the P226 in my hands. It was dark, and about the only sound was the creak of the ancient wood as I climbed. The landing was a broad dogleg with a dark wooden banister. There were five doors. All of them stood partially open. Four of them were bedrooms. They had the drapes closed and were in darkness. The fifth was a bathroom, and pale evening light filtered through the opaque frosted glass of the window.

We checked each room in turn. Each was a mess. The wardrobes were open, and those that were built in had the back panels ripped out. The chests of drawers had been emptied and the larger ones partially smashed. All the bedding had been dumped on the floor, and the mattresses and pillows had been ripped to shreds.

In the bathroom, the cistern had its lid removed, and the side of the bathtub had been smashed and torn away.

Gallin holstered her BUL and leaned on the doorjamb. "You think they found it?"

"I have no idea, but we have to assume they did."

She nodded. "You figure we have anything left to do here?"

"Not unless he buried it in the garden. I doubt Sir Lacklan's boys could be any more thorough than these guys have been." I paused to give a fairly heartfelt sigh. "I'll tell you one thing, though."

"What?"

"They didn't touch the floorboards."

She frowned at me. Then slowly her face started to clear. "Floorboards would be an obvious place to look..."

I nodded. "If they didn't get to them, it means they had stopped looking. Either they were interrupted, or, more likely, they had found what they were looking for."

"Son of a bitch."

"Okay, let's go talk to Mrs. Sunny."

London is not built on the grid system. The streets of London are more like a bowl of noodles. They have evolved since the Stone Age, when they were regular paths between settlements and the river, and they twist and bend and wind according to where the changing needs of history have led Londoners' feet. So though Mrs. Sunny's house was just seven miles from Walm Lane, it took us the better part of an hour to reach it on Moravian Street in the East End. So evening was turning to night and the streetlamps were glowing dull amber by the time we got there.

Moravian Street is short and ugly, the houses are small and ugly, and they have no front or back yards. The woman we had come to think of as Mrs. Sunny, though that was not her name, lived at Number 4. It was a small, redbrick box with a black door and a window behind which the drapes closed. We managed to park outside, and while Gallin killed the engine and climbed out, I rang the doorbell.

I saw the curtain twitch, and after a moment, the door opened a couple of inches on a chain. A woman whom the gods had blessed with few graces peered out at us. What we could see of her was pale pink, though when she spoke, her teeth were a deep, funeral amber. She said, "What?"

Gallin spoke as I was drawing breath. "Good evening. I am not sure if we have the right place. We have some money we need to deliver to Sunny. Is he your husband?"

She thought about it for all of three seconds.

"Money? What money?"

"He did some work for us." Gallin glanced at me. "Some, uh, research. And we wanted to pay him. It's only a few grand. We can come back some other time when it's more convenient—"

"No."

"No?"

"It's convenient now. Who'd you say you were?"

"We'd rather talk inside."

"How many grand?"

"Five."

She didn't look impressed, so I leaned forward and said, "And perhaps another two in gratitude for your help?"

She eyed me up and down. "You a Yank?"

"I am indeed. Benjamin Franklin at your service. May we come in?"

The door closed, and a moment later opened again to release the smell of boiled cabbage in a short, narrow hallway with a kitchen at the end and an open door on the right through which you could hear the sound of a TV. The people on that TV were laughing, though there didn't seem to be much to laugh at.

"You'd better come in then," she said with her unsettling amber smile.

We crammed ourselves into the hallway, and she ushered us through into a small living room with two small sofas, a TV, and a gas imitation coal fire.

"You want some tea? I can make a cup."

We shook our heads and smiled as we sat. I said, "You are very kind, Mrs., ahh..."

"Robertson, like the jam."

Gallin gave me a smile and said, "Jelly."

"I know. Jelly is jam, and Jell-O is jelly." I looked at Mrs. Robertson and went on, "But we are fine, thank you. We won't take up much of your time. Please, sit. Now we just need to confirm that we have the right person. Sunny is of course his nickname..." I creased my face into a grin and gave a small laugh. She didn't reciprocate. She just said, "Sami, S-

A-M-I. He's from Iran." She pronounced it *eye-ran*. "Sami Fikri."

Gallin pointed at her and said, "But you are Robertson."

"Kept me own name. I wasn't going to be called Fikri, was I? Can you imagine? Mrs. Fikri? I'd be a right bloody laughin' stock, wouldn't I? Mavis flamin' Fikri. I ask you. I only married him 'cause he got me in the family way." She turned to Gallin, like being a woman she would understand. "You're stuck then, aren't you? What can you do? You've got his baby, you got to flippin' marry him, aincha?"

Gallin blinked like she had several alternative suggestions in her mind but didn't want to express them. Instead she said, "Right. So the work we need to pay him for is when he helped out with those four guys—"

I added, "Rashid, Mohamed, Omar, and Hassan."

She nodded. "Yeah." We all stared at each other and, sensing that more was expected from her, she added, "Up in Willesden."

"Exactly. So we've been trying to get in touch with him so we could pay him, but he seems to have gone AWOL. Any idea where he is?"

She shifted her ass on the sofa like she wasn't really comfortable with that question. I glanced doubtfully at Gallin, then back at Mavis. "I mean, I guess it's okay to give you the money for him, and a little extra for your help, but we have more work we want him to do, and it would be nice to be able to talk to him in person, you know?"

Gallin nodded at her. "Better for everyone all round."

"Well," she said, "he gets around a bit, know what I mean? He's always coming and going, up and down, in and

SON OF HELL | 61

out." She laughed suddenly, like up and down and in and out were funny.

I smiled more, hunched my shoulders, and spread my hands. "Hey! If you can't help, you can't help, right? Thanks for talking to us, anyway. When you see him, tell him we tried to pay him." I went to stand. Gallin stood. Mavis flamin' Fikri Robertson said, "Oh, well, no! I suppose I could probably get a message to him."

"When?" Gallin asked then smiled.

"Umm..."

"You know how it is. We're on a kind of deadline."

"Umm..."

"Say tonight, nine p.m., ten p.m.?"

"I, umm..."

I said, "I'll tell you what we're going to do, Mavis. We are going to go. We are going to get a down payment on Sunny's next job, and we are going to come back in a couple of hours. In that time, you be a trooper, find Sunny, and tell him we really need to see him and we have lots of money for him—and also for you. Call it a finder's fee. How does that sound to you, Mavis?"

She swallowed, then nodded. "Yeah, sounds all right."

Gallin winked at her. "Like Schwarzenegger, we'll be back."

Mavis gave a titter that sounded slightly scared and saw us to the door.

In the car, speeding through the crowded, nocturnal streets of London, toward the Temple, Gallin asked, "Was it Sunny? Did he ransack the house?"

I didn't answer. I was thinking hard.

"Whatever the answer is," she went on, "it raises two

more questions. One, if it was, where is he now? That's an important one because he may not be in the UK. Two, if it *wasn't* him, who the hell was it?"

"Whoever set up this operation in the first place."

"That's who Sunny works for, right? So if I am the guy Sunny works for, I am going to tell Sunny to recover that evidence, because we are going to need it when we come at the UK at the International Court of Justice in the Hague, right?" She looked at me earnestly. "Am I right?"

"You're right, but that raises another question. Two questions. First, how did the Russians, or Sunny, or whoever the hell it was, how did they know that Rashid had that evidence? And, second, how did they know he had hidden it?"

She was quiet for a long time. I knew what she was thinking, and she said it as we pulled up outside Sir Lacklan's office.

"Answer that," she said, "and you answer who killed Rashid and the others in Ukraine."

She killed the engine, and I nodded at her. "Right."

When we got into Sir Lacklan's office, Gabriel was there. Gallin went and gave him a kiss, and I sat. When Gallin had taken a chair, Sir Lacklan spoke. "This is an almighty mess. The PM is having kittens, and I don't blame him. Berlin and Paris are saying they simply cannot afford to get involved in a conflict with Russia." He gave a dry, humorless laugh. "I mean, the reality is that over twenty percent of young French men are immigrants or refugees who will not take up arms to protect France. In Germany, the situation is much the same, as it is across the European Union. They are very clear. If

Russia pushes ahead with this, they will not back us militarily.

"And we all know the United State's position, whether Mr. Trump gets in or not. If the Russians allege an act of war, and prove it at the ICJ, and decide to retaliate, we are royally screwed." He paused and took a deep breath. "So before we start, has anyone any news? Preferably good news, please."

I said, "Yeah, but it's not great. It pretty much confirms your earlier assessment. We went to the house on Walm Lane where Rashid and his buddies stayed and did their alleged training. The place had been torn apart. Sofa, chairs, cushions, mattresses—everything had been torn apart."

Gabriel muttered, "But we don't know if they found anything."

Gallin shook her head. "We think they might have. They didn't pull up any of the floorboards. That means they stopped looking for some reason."

Sir Lacklan sighed heavily through his nose. "Then, as you say, we have to assume they found Rashid's pictures and videos. But we are no closer to knowing where Nepel and Sunny's evidence is."

I said, "On the way here, we paid a visit to Sunny's wife. He is Sami—S-A-M-I—Fikri from Iran. They are married, but she kept her name Robertson, because she wasn't going to be called Fikri. In her words, she'd be 'a right bloody laughin' stock—Mavis flamin' Fikri.'"

Gabriel sniggered. Sir Lacklan raised an eyebrow. "Thank you for that, Alex. Did you learn anything, err, *useful?*"

"Yeah, she confirmed he'd been missing. We knew that, but we also found that she could contact him. Which might mean he hasn't left the country yet. We told her to tell him we had money for him and a new job. We needed to talk to him, and we would go back later tonight to see what he had said."

He nodded. "A forlorn hope, perhaps, but worth a try."

"At the moment, it's pretty much all we've got. One thing that's playing on my mind is why he's disappeared. Did he hear about Rashid and the others and fears he's next? If that is the case, then it's possible somebody else was supposed to collect the evidence, and he got there first in an attempt to get himself some insurance. That might give us a small ray of hope."

Gabriel grunted, and Sir Lacklan drew breath. Gallin interrupted both of them.

"Sir Lacklan, there is something I don't understand, and maybe you could clarify it for me. Why is the SIS not present at this meeting? Russia is directly accusing SIS—MI6—of orchestrating the terrorist attack in Moscow. They should be here. They were at the SAS base in Ukraine, in the shape of George Locke, supervising our interrogations. Why are they not here, sharing what they know with us? For that matter, the same applies to MI5."

He was quiet for several moments, looking at his long, boney hands on his desk, and I began to wonder whether he was going to reply at all. Finally he drew breath again and said, "I have spoken to the directors of both MI5 and the SIS, and I have spoken to the minister. We all agree that, until we can establish whether there is a breach somewhere, it is best if we remain as compartmentalized as is possible. Need to know."

"So the United Kingdom's minister for defence and the head of the British branch of ODIN are more comfortable speaking to the Mossad than to their own intelligence departments?"

Sir Lacklan's cheeks flushed. "That is not what I said, Captain—"

Before he could continue, I cut in. "I get that as far as our sharing intelligence with them is concerned. But what about any intelligence they can share with us?"

"I am afraid there is precious little. You met George Locke in Ukraine. He has obviously become a person of interest after the assassination of the prisoners, and SIS has closed ranks until they have conducted their own internal inquiry."

I looked at Gallin's dad. "Gabriel?"

"I am afraid we have very little to add. Of course, it is as you said before to Sir Lacklan: These were people who came onto our radar almost as a matter of protocol: four Islamic men who arrived more or less together and had never been here before, except for Rashid, who was already known as an Islamic activist. But we had no way of connecting them with what was going to happen in Moscow." He nodded a few times, looking into space. "But we did our due diligence and noted that while they were at Walm Lane, the man known as Sunny—"

"Sami Fikri."

"Thank you. That Sami Fikri, Sunny, went twice to Brussels and then the Hague."

Sir Lacklan looked at me and then at Gallin. "Find Sami Fikri, catch him, do whatever you need to do—take him into international waters to do it if you have to—*but find out where that evidence is!*"

SEVEN

THE APARTMENT WAS EXCESSIVELY LUXURIOUS. Colonel Alexandrina Vitsin despised luxury. Vladimir had insisted that a representative of Russia must display opulence and luxury to uphold the status of the country, but to her, this opulence, this luxury, was a sign of weakness, a deep, inner weakness that consumed the body—the body physical and the body politic—from within, dissolving it into flab and then slime.

The image of slime lingered a moment in her mind. She sucked on her cigarette, taking the smoke deep into her lungs and trailing it from her nose as she moved to the large terrace that overlooked the Ravin du Bois de la Cambre park. Dusk was quickening into evening. The lights were winking on below, and the traffic reached her as a sigh, perhaps a protracted whisper. Her thoughts, however, were not on the park or the elegant streets of Brussels. Her thoughts were on the president.

She had admired Vladimir Putin for many years—for

decades, in fact. When he was young and insecure, an unknown from the KGB taking his first, faltering steps in power, she had encouraged him, advised him, initiated him into the doctrines of temporal power. He had been able, ruthless, and committed. His focus had been extraordinary. But he had always had that weakness: his vanity. Always he had been seduced by the trappings of power as much as by the power itself. It was as though for him, the power without the trappings had no meaning.

That was his weakness.

And Russia, the great bear, was rotting, her guts dissolving into slime, while Vladimir Putin, who could have been so great—who *should* have been so great—now turned also to slime himself, crazed, psychotic, obsessed with the show, ignoring the substance.

She thought of his catastrophic failures in Ukraine and curled her lip. He needed to be replaced, but by whom? A return to the spineless Medvedev? Patrushev?

A cool breeze touched her face and made her shudder.

There were possibilities, but none excited her. When she recognized his replacement, when she knew who, then she would act. Putin, who had been so thrilling and dangerous in the beginning, was now a decrepit, slobbering fool who needed to die.

Her thoughts returned to Ukraine, an invasion that should have taken two weeks, a territory they would desperately need in the future, and it had degenerated into a farce that had humiliated Russia in the eyes of the world. They had been saved from total humiliation by the decrepit stupidity of the Western leaders, which was greater still than Vladimir's.

There was a ring at the bell. She turned from the terrace and stepped into the broad drawing room with its suede sofa, vast armchairs, and copper fireplace. Two genuine Picassos hung on the walls. Before she left, she planned to burn holes in them with a cigarette.

She flicked ash on the beige carpet and smiled as she trod it into the pure wool fabric with her toe. It was one of the things she liked and admired in herself: her complete lack of respect. For anything.

A tall man in a well-cut dark blue suit stepped into the room. He was Igor. He had a shaved head and blue eyes that had become accustomed to being indifferent to the suffering and death of others.

"It is Nepel, Colonel."

She didn't speak. She gave a slight upward jerk of her chin, and he turned away. After some thirty seconds, a short man with too much hair, heavy glasses, and a dense, red beard entered the room. He stopped, gave a sloppy, ineffectual bow, and said, "Colonel, a pleasure to see you again."

He spoke the accentless English of a good grammar school but lacked the elegant drawl of the better private schools which the English called public schools. He did not speak Russian. He had been denied that so that his integration would be perfect. He was able and useful, and highly intelligent, but Colonel Vitsin despised him and would have enjoyed seeing him weep.

"Sit," she told him.

He sat in one of the armchairs. She remained standing. As she sucked on her cigarette and removed it from her mouth, he noticed the tips of her fingers and her lips were stained brown by the nicotine.

"They are dead?"

"I killed them myself."

"What about the evidence you and Sunny collected?"

"Sunny has it. It emerged also under interrogation that though Rashid and the others were so angry at our recording and photographing them, they themselves kept a photographic and video record of their stay. Though they were careful to cover their faces."

"Why you didn't know about this? Why Sunny didn't know?"

"They kept it secret until the team of agents in Ukraine questioned them. They were quite skilled, and finally Rashid told the American that they had made a photographic and video record."

"Where is that?"

"Sunny recovered it. Rashid had hidden it behind the panels of the bathtub."

"You said the American agent. They are not both American?"

"No, Colonel. One is American, and the other has dual English Israeli nationality. They are both very effective."

Vitsin's eyes narrowed to slits.

"What are their names, these agents?"

"Alex Mason is the American. The female is Captain Aila Gallin. He was a bit vague about what department he worked for. He said loosely it was a department of the Pentagon, but I got the impression it was Central Intelligence. She works for the Mossad."

"Alex Mason."

Her tone made Nepel frown. "You know him?"

"I know him. Kill him and the woman Aila Gallin. Be

careful; they are both very dangerous. Kill them both. Do they know you are Nepel?"

He gave a thin smile. "Everybody suspects George Locke."

"Soon they will know. We have little time. I need the evidence here tomorrow. And Mason and Gallin dead."

"I'll see to it straight away."

"Go."

Nepel was nothing if not good at pretending to be obedient. He stood, smiled, gave a small bow, and left.

Down in the parking garage, he climbed into a neutral euro-car that might have been a Seat Ibiza or a Volkswagen Golf and drove out onto Lloyd George Avenue. As he came out into the traffic, he said, "Siri, call Joseph."

The phone rang three times, and a pleasant voice answered, "Hey, Neil, how's it hanging?"

"Pendulous, old chap. Listen, I need you to find the two agents who have been put on the Ukraine terrorist case."

"Mason and Gallin."

"That's them."

"Yeah, we've been watching them. We have a team on them. They were at Sunny's wife's place a while ago."

"Really? Any sign of him?"

"Not yet."

"Okay, don't worry about him for now. Find out where they are and kill them."

"Oh." Joseph sounded vaguely surprised. "Okay. Accident, mugging, act of God...?"

"I don't care. I'm actually on my way to do it myself. So if you can take me to them and have them all lined up, all to the good. But if you get the chance to take them out before I get there, so much the better. Do it."

"Cool. I'll tell the boys."

"Love you, man."

"Yeah, hang loose."

By the time Nepel had arrived at the airport to catch his flight to London, his beard and abundant hair were gone, as were his heavy glasses, and by the time he emerged from the toilets, his blue eyes had turned brown and the passport in his back pocket was American and in the name of Allan Bloom.

Back in her apartment, Colonel Alexandrina Vitsin sat at the long dining table turning a packet of cigarettes in circles.

Nero.

She had been pursuing him for years across the world. She had had him. She had been so close. Alexandrina had hated most people since her mother had taught her the power of hate. Some people she hated more than others, some she loathed with a passion—though most of those were now dead and grateful for the liberation. She smiled a private smile. But Nero. With Nero, it was a passion that had become like a black hole. It was a place of darkness. She needed his pain like she needed air. She needed to see his weeping. She needed hear his beseeching, his begging for death, for release from her cruelty and her power. And finally, she needed his complete annihilation.

Alexandrina Vitsin did not believe there was such a thing as a soul. But if there was one, she wanted Nero's soul annihilated too. She would gladly die to pursue his soul to hell and destroy it.

The pack stopped revolving, and she shook a black

cigarette loose. As she poked it in her mouth, she noticed that her fingers were trembling. She put the flame to the cylinder and sucked hard so that the tip glowed. She could smell Nero's presence. She could feel him, and she knew with a certainty that was absolute that soon, very soon, she would hold him pressed to her and feel his life fade.

That made her smile. She chuckled. It made her want to laugh out loud.

EIGHT

By the time we got back to Mavis flamin' Fikri's house, it was past eleven, and a London drizzle had set in, painting the blacktop with silver streaks and here and there, liquid red, green, and amber. I climbed out, turned up my collar, and rang the bell, while Gallin came up beside me, gripping the collar of her leather jacket held up in her left hand, and her right hand shoved down in her pocket. The drapes twitched as they had before, and a moment later, the door opened.

"*Come in, come in!*" She hissed it impatiently, beckoning at us with her hand, peering behind and beyond us. We stepped over the threshold, and she hustled us into the living room. We sat where we had sat before, and she sat on the edge of the sofa with her hands laid flat on her lap.

"Who'd you say you were?"

Gallin and I glanced at each other. I said, "We didn't, Mrs. Robertson. I will be honest with you because I can see you are an intelligent woman who has both feet firmly on the ground. We think—" I paused, made a kind of wince, and nodded. "We are pretty sure that Sunny has got himself into a spot of trouble, and we want to help him."

Her eyes narrowed. "What kind of trouble?"

I smiled. I pointed at her and turned the smile on Gallin. "See? Didn't I tell you?" I turned back to Mavis, who was herself repressing a smile. "I told her. I said, 'Captain Gallin, there are no flies on that Mavis, I'll tell you that for nothing.' We don't know exactly what kind of trouble, Mavis. But I think you *do* know what kind of trouble. I think it's serious, and I think he is in serious need of money. Am I far wrong?"

She studied my face for a long moment with a couple of quick glances thrown at Gallin. She was calculating. The cash register was working.

"No," she said. "You're not wrong. But he doesn't know who he can trust. And neither do I. I was going to say, how do I know you're who you say you are? But then I realized, you ain't told me yet who you are."

I reached in my pocket and pulled out my wallet. From it I extracted an ID card that said I worked for the Pentagon at the Office of the Director of Intelligence. She studied it for a while, like she'd be able to tell if it was a fake, and when she handed it back, Gallin handed her a card that said she worked for MI5.

She looked at that a moment, then studied Gallin's face. "MI5," she said.

"We and the Brits are cooperating," I told her, then gave a comfortable smile. "Whatever the politicians get up to, we, the guys who do all the work, we stay close, and we cooperate a lot. That's the real special relationship. So we are cooperating with MI5 at the moment because we believe there is a real threat from Moscow. We think that Sunny was cheated and drawn in to a web of lies and deceit, and before he knew it, he was trapped and didn't know how to get out. Am I right?"

She nodded. "He don't tell me much, but that was pretty much it. Something like that."

I went on. "Some guys were killed. Guys he knew, friends of his whom he had worked with. And I think that spooked him, and he decided to disappear. Am I wrong?"

"No."

"We, Mavis, we are looking for the guys who killed those boys, and we want to protect Sunny from coming to harm. You've spoken to him?"

"Yes."

"What did he tell you?"

"He said if I thought you was on the level, I should take the money you give me and give you a message about where you could meet him. Then you talk to him, and he'll see if he thinks you're on the level."

I spread my hands and gave her my open, honest face.

"Are we on the level?"

"I don't know. But I suppose we won't know until we put it to the test, will we?"

"Nope. I guess not. So where can we meet him?"

"Cittie of York. It's an old pub on High Holborn, where it meets Chancery Lane. As you go in, there are booths on the righthand side. He'll be in one of the booths."

I looked at Gallin. She nodded. "I know it. It's a nice pub."

I stood. "Okay, let's go."

Mavis watched me get to my feet and said, "What about me dosh?"

I pulled out my wallet and handed her a thousand pounds sterling. "You'll get the other half if all goes to plan."

She gave a smile that was, in the words of Dire Straits, all greasy with the money, and said, "I knew you was a gentleman. Close the door on your way out, won't you?"

It was not far to High Holborn from Mavis' place, and though parking in London is like trying to solve the mysteries of quantum physics with a blunt pencil and a calculator with no batteries, we got lucky and found a multistory parking garage down an alley opposite the Cittie of York pub.

We left the car and hunched through the drizzle among the slow-moving traffic and pushed into the warmth of the pub. Brits talk quietly, but get enough of them together in a pub and you get a warm hum of conversation and laughter. The booths were on the right, as Mavis had said, and at the far end was a big iron stove with burning logs inside it. The place was filling up but not yet crowded.

We walked along the booths looking for an Iranian guy sitting alone. We found him about halfway down. He looked straight at us, and there was fear concealed behind his lack of expression. His short hair was dark, and his eyes were large and almost black, but his skin was pale. I leaned on the entrance to the booth.

"Sunny?"

He took a few seconds over answering, then said, "Who wants to know?"

"Me." I pointed to Gallin. "And her. I'm Alex, she is Aila, and I think your wife told you we were coming to meet you." I stood aside to let Gallin slide in and slid in after her. "Mind if we join you?"

His face was sour. "Would it make any difference if I did?"

Gallin sighed and rubbed her face with her palms. I said, "Now, Sunny, it seems to me that for a man in your position, you are kind of taking the wrong attitude. See, I know you are afraid. I know you are afraid that whoever recruited you, whoever gave you that job in Willesden, now wants you dead." I gave my head a twitch. "Or worse, wants you alive. And I have to say, I think you are probably right."

I leaned back, and Gallin waved a finger, indicating me and her. "Us?" she said. "The big advantage you have with us, Sunny, is that we don't actually care whether you are dead or alive, but we are willing to trade with you, if you have something that we want. In exchange for what we want, we can give you something that *you* want, like, say, the next fifty years of your life."

He nodded. "Yeah, that's funny. No, seriously. You're a funny woman. I really want to laugh now. I'll tell you something else funny." He leaned forward and echoed Gallin's gesture with his own hand, indicating me and her. "What if you two clowns are the actual bastards you say you want to protect me from?"

I said, "Do we look Russian to you?"

He shook his head. "No, you look and sound like a Yank, and she looks Spanish or Italian, but then bloody Nepel didn't look or sound very Russian either. He looked and sounded like a bloody toff."

I looked at Gallin. "A toff?"

"English upper class, probably Oxford or Cambridge via Eton or Harrow public schools."

"Public schools are upper class here?"

"They are private and very expensive, but we call them public."

"Are you two done with the multicultural education?"

He was looking at us like we were insane, which I guess was justified at the time.

I said, "So Nepel seemed to be British upper class?"

"English. It's not the same. And yeah, he did. Like she said, Eaton Oxford type."

Gallin frowned. "It didn't seem strange to you that an upper class Englishman was orchestrating an Islamic attack on Russia?"

"No, not really. It seemed to me to be a logical thing to do, and in fact I wondered why they never done it before. Israel are our allies, right? Iran has been hammering Israel for decades, and all her bloody allies do is tell her to show restraint. Now Russia comes along and starts invading Ukraine. *Her* allies fail to help *her*, and then Russia goes and makes an alliance with flamin' Iran! So is it a smart move to try and bring Russia and Iran into conflict with each other? Yeah, it's a good idea."

Gallin said, "I thought you were a Muslim. You don't talk like a Muslim."

He studied her face a moment, then said suddenly, "You're a Jew. Well, let me tell you something. If you grow up in London, with your eyes open, there is no way you can keep your faith, whatever it is. I don't care if it's Christian, Jewish, Islamic, or any other kind of faith. You know why? Because there are too many people asking too many questions that have no answer. The only way you keep your faith in this city is if you keep your eyes shut!" He sat back, staring at Gallin. "But you're a Jew. Aila, Aila Gallin. That's a Jewish name. My wife said you was a captain. You been in the IDF, haven't you?"

She glanced at me. We had both sensed the same opportunity. She said, "You do keep your eyes open, don't you? Yes, I did my time in the IDF, and now I work for the Mossad."

She reached in her pocket and pulled out her ID card, the real one, and tossed it across the table. He picked it up and looked at it, then handed it back, looked at me, and nodded.

"That makes more sense." He laughed suddenly and unexpectedly. "The US squirming in the tortuous position of not knowing whose arse to kiss. Should you kiss the oil rich Arabs' arses, who have done so much to make the Clintons and the Obamas so very happy and rich, or should you kiss the arses of the Jewish and Israeli bankers who own the Federal Reserve? How to keep them both happy? So here you are, the Pentagon and the Mossad, dashing to rescue me from...who?" He shrugged his shoulders and shook his head. "MI6?" He laughed again, but more softly. "That's a bit freaky, isn't it? The CIA and the Mossad joined together to save a lapsed Muslim from MI6! I bet you never thought you'd live to see *that* day!"

"Yeah, it wasn't in my weekly Scorpio horoscope on Monday. But now that you have uncovered our dark secret, maybe you can use that fine brain of yours to take the next step."

He stared at me a moment, then drained what was left of

his pint. As he set down the empty glass, he smacked his lips. "You're not the people who killed Rashid and his mates in Ukraine. Because however bloody weird the interests of the UK, the US, and the EU may be these days, Israel's interests are very clear and simple. They are the ones they have always had: survival. Which means the one nation on the planet that really does not want a war between Britain and Russia is Israel. Because if that happens, the alliances that keep Israel safe start to crumble." He pointed at me. "And you represent that faction of the United States that is aligned with Israel."

I nodded. "And..."

"So in theory, you don't want me dead. You want me alive to give you those photos and the videos—and testimony, if it comes to that."

Gallin nodded. "Right, Sunny. Put briefly, we are the closest thing you have to friends right now."

He tipped his empty glass and stared into it. "Who's a lucky boy, then?"

"Are we done fencing?" She watched him till he nodded. "Start talking. And try to say something useful."

He turned his big, sour eyes on me. For a moment, I thought they were the eyes of a man who'd been raised on promises he was too smart to believe but not smart enough to find an alternative to.

"She's nice, isn't she? It's the same with all the bloody Israelis I've met. They're all so bloody intense."

"We are not hanging out here, Sami. We're on the clock."

He sighed. "All right. There's two packages. One is the lot Nepel put together. It's a bunch of videos and photographs of Rashid Patel, he was Pakistani but born and bred here in London. He was a wanker, Allah this and Allah bleedin' that. Then there was Mohamed Hussein. He was from Iraq and basically just did what he was told. I think Nepel had threatened to kill his wife and kids if he didn't. Poor bastard just wanted to go home and tend his goats. Then there was Omar bin Abbas, French but originally from Syria. I don't think he was particularly religious. He just liked killing. And finally there was Hassan from Afghanistan. Didn't talk much. He was just doing what they told him was God's will. He never asked them how they *knew* it was God's will. He just did what he was told, like Mohamed."

I asked, "How compelling is this stuff?"

"Pretty compelling. Rashid got really pissed off about it. He said it was unprofessional and put his boys at risk. He told Mohamed, Omar, and Hassan to keep their faces covered at all times when Nepel was around. Even so, I think one or two got through. There's one where they're all standing in a row outside the house on Walm Lane, in Willesden. And there's a couple of videos he took without them knowing, where he kind of engineered a conversation about how the alliance between Russia and Iran was the work of the Great Satan. It's pretty bad stuff, and Nepel, like I told you, he is totally English upper class establishment."

Gallin said, "You said there were two packages."

He lifted his glass to show us. "Do you mind?"

Gallin said, "I'll get them."

I slid out of the booth. She squeezed out and made her way to the bar. As I slipped back in, he said, "I fuckin' hate religion. Do you know why I married my wife? I don't love her. Who could love that, right? Not even her mother. Don't get me wrong. I'm fond of her. She's loyal. But you couldn't get romantic about her, could you? You've seen her. No, I married her to get at my imam at the mosque. I married an infidel to poke him in the eye. I read once—" He reached for his glass, remembered it was empty, and sighed. "I read that the most moral people in the world were the atheists, you know why?"

"I know you're going to tell me."

He shook his head. "Nah, forget it. Why would you care?"

For a moment I felt bad. "I'm sorry. Tell me. I think I can guess, but tell me."

He eyed me a moment with his sour eyes. "Because they have to take responsibility for the things they do and say. They can't pass the buck to a god." He looked away from me into his empty glass where traces of foam clung to the edges and spoke half to himself. "Men should be responsible for the things they do and say."

I was quiet for a bit, watching him. Finally as Gallin approached through the thickening crowd, holding three pints of dark, nut brown bitter, I said, "I agree."

She put them on the table, I got out of the way, and we took up our positions again. When we were settled, I said, "Before we get on to the second package, where is that package now?"

He picked up his glass, pulled off a quarter, and wiped his mouth on the back of his left hand as he set down the glass.

"I have it," he said.

NINE

I felt a hot pellet in my gut. "You want to be clear about that?"

"I have it in my possession. Not here. Not now. I am not that stupid. But I have that evidence. I know where it is and how to get hold of it."

"How much is it going to cost me for you to hand it over?"

"Not as much as you might think. I might be a spineless bastard, which I am, but this ain't a bad country. If the bloody politicians would just lay off, it would be a good place to live. So I don't want England massacred by the Russians. But I don't want to be hunted down and killed by jihadists, either. So Mavis is left out of this and I disappear into the FBI's witness protection program, or something similar, and a million bucks to start a new life. In exchange I give you that package and the other one, and I am available to answer any questions I can. Fair?"

I glanced at Gallin. She raised her shoulders an eighth of an inch.

I said, "Tell me about the second package. You have that too?"

"Yes."

Gallin asked, "How'd you get it?"

"I had a hunch Rashid had hidden the stuff in the house in Willesden. I tore the place apart and found it eventually behind the bath panel."

"Okay, tell us about this package. What does it contain?"

"Rashid was disgusted by Nepel's apparent sloppy security and lack of protocol. He took photos and films of his own, on the advice of his imam. They were careful always to hide their faces so they could always deny it was them. But what they could do, with those pictures and that footage, was prove that it was MI6 who arranged the operation. He could sense something was wrong, but he couldn't imagine how wrong."

I took my first pull on my pint of Sam Smith's Yorkshire Bitter. It's not like anything else on the planet. There is practically no fizz. It's like drinking roasted nuts with a side order of beef thrown in.

I set down the glass and wiped my mouth. "I can almost guarantee that we will get the okay to go ahead with your terms. Obviously I need to confirm it with my superior. Meantime I would suggest we take you to a Mossad safe house where we can protect you."

I glanced at Gallin. She nodded. "I can arrange that."

I gave him something close to a smile. "At least they'll want you alive. Meantime, you need to get the goods and be ready to hand them over when we next meet. If you get nervous, Sunny, just remember we need your live testimony as much as everything else."

"Okay." He gave a single nod.

"So where and when?"

He thought for a moment. "You know Ladbroke Grove? Portobello Road?"

"Sure."

"Tomorrow they have the market there. The place is crawling with people. Right at the north end, practically at the top, you have a small street called Raddington Road. Be there at eleven a.m. with a vehicle. If you have access to an armored Land Rover, so much the better. And I am not joking."

"We can probably swing that." Gallin nodded. "I can get one."

"You pull up at the corner of Raddington Road and Blagrove Road. Don't worry if you don't see me. I won't look like me. I'll look like a tramp or a wino or something. Leave the rear right door open so I can climb in the back, and we move off."

I said, "Tomorrow, corner of Raddington and Blagrove, eleven a.m., rear right door ready for you to climb in." I looked at Gallin. "Good?"

"Good. No problem." She jerked her chin at him. "One more thing. We know this is coming from Moscow and Tehran, though probably mainly Moscow. Did Nepel give any indication of how far up it went or who was involved?"

He screwed up his face. "Kind of, but not really. He said it went right to the top. I don't know how true it was, but he suggested Putin himself was involved personally. But mainly he said the brains behind it was a Russian colonel. I think it was a woman 'cause he used to call her the crazy bitch."

"Where is Nepel now?"

"I have no idea. He just vanished. No trace. I haven't really tried to contact him, but his phone, email, all that stuff is just gone. Like it never existed."

"Okay." I nodded. "We're going to go. Give us a while before you leave. You stay safe."

He didn't say anything. We slipped out of the booth and pushed through the warm, laughing crowd and out into the dark drizzle.

The traffic had thinned out. A black cab passed with its yellow light shining warm, promising home. A big red bus followed, and we loped across the road with our collars up. At the other side, we moved down the dark, unlit alley toward the parking garage.

Ahead of us on the righthand side of the road, there was a car parked. It was dark, but my instinct made me step out into the road so I was between the car and Gallin. In my peripheral vision, I saw her reach behind her back for her piece. That was when the front passenger door of the car opened and a guy who right then was just a big, dark shadow got out, stood erect, and turned to face us. He must have been six-six and built like a bison. He had on a big, dark coat and spoke in a deep baritone that said he was from the Caribbean.

He said, "Excuse me, sir."

As he said it, the driver's door opened, and another guy in a dark coat climbed out. Something about the way his right arm hung, something about the way he didn't use it to get out of the vehicle, I knew he was holding a piece. I smiled and stepped to one side so he was between me and his pal.

"How can I help you?"

He pulled a leather wallet from his pocket and let it drop open to reveal an invisible badge. He said "Detective Inspector Smith, CID. Are you Mr. Alex Mason and Captain Aila Gallin?"

The other guy was coming up behind him, walking not fast but purposeful. I said, "Yes" and watched the farthest guy's shoulders hunch as he raised his weapon to fire over the big guy's shoulder. I didn't think. I acted out of instinct. My left arm wrapped around Gallin's shoulders, and I dragged her to me, out of the line of fire, and simultaneously I smashed my right instep into a place no man's instep should ever be smashed. The big guy wheezed and folded.

As my boot came down, I twisted on the ball of my foot and drove a savage hook through his jaw. There was a *phut!* And a *smack!* And a shower of redbrick dust and shards erupted from where Gallin's head had been seconds before. Now she slipped from under my arm and bobbed up on my right. She had her arms stretched out in front of her and the BUL pumping out three rounds that made an awful mess of the gunman's head and neck.

The big guy hit the blacktop, and we both saw the rear doors of the car opening. There were inarticulate shouts and curses. Gallin snapped at me, "*Go!*" and she was gone, streaking ahead of me into the shadows of the parking garage. I followed and heard two pairs of running feet behind me.

We sprinted through the ill-lit grime of the garage. I saw Gallin head for the steel door that led to the elevator and followed her in. As she ran up the stairs, I saw her fitting a suppressor to the BUL. Her face was completely impassive. I heard the door slam beneath us and feet tramping up the concrete steps. We came to the third floor where we had left the Jag. She pushed out through that door and stepped around the corner to her right. I ran and took cover beside a Range Rover about twelve or fifteen feet away. It gave me a good angle on the door.

We waited, and after thirty seconds, the door opened. There were two guys there. Tall and big, but these two were not Caribbean. They had their weapons in front of them, but they didn't step through. Then Gallin did one of those things that make her special. She pressed the key fob to her Jag. The lights flashed and it bleeped, and they ran through, thinking we were getting away. She shot the first guy in the back of the knee, and I shot the second one in the head.

He fell on his face without bending and hit the floor with an ugly thud. Gallin was already walking to the guy who was clutching his leg and whimpering. She hunkered down by his head.

"Who sent you?"

"Screw you!"

"I won't kill you, wiseass. I'll blow your other knee off. I am not a nice person. Who sent you to kill us?"

He moved too fast to follow. It was half a second. He reached out with his right hand and grasped her wrist. Next thing his thumb was on her finger on the trigger and he'd blown a hole right through his own head. Gallin cursed violently, wrenching her hand out of his as his feet jerked and quivered.

"God *dammit!*"

I grabbed her arm. "Come on, we've got to get out of here."

"Son of a *bitch!*"

She said it as we started running. Next thing, she had slipped behind the wheel. I slammed my door, and we were cruising sedately down the ramps to the exit. We paid, which seemed to take several hours, and then we rolled out of the garage. We had to go up on the sidewalk to get past the body in the road, and as we approached the intersection with High Holborn, I saw the big guy hobbling along knock-kneed, leaning against the wall.

We turned left toward West London, and after a couple of minutes cruising behind red taillights, she said, "Colonel Alexandrina Vitsin."

I gave a single nod. "That's what I thought. A Russian colonel who was a woman you could call the crazy bitch. There can't be two like that, huh?"

She gave her head a sideways twitch. "In Russia? Don't know what to tell you, Mason."

"It's her, Gallin. I can feel the disturbance in the Force. We shouldn't have let her go in Spain. That woman is as subtle as a greased snake with tentacles. She's gotten into the SIS, and from there she is reaching out into ODIN."

She nodded. "I'll give you that. The setup here is leaking like a colander. They not only knew we would be there, but they knew our names. Is it Sir Lacklan?"

I thought about it and winced at the idea. "I doubt it, but we can't know for sure. You and I haven't been in contact with many people besides him, but we don't know who he talks to after we leave."

"He's not stupid. I can't see him—"

"No, I agree, Gallin. But on the other hand, there are people he *has* to talk to, whether he likes it or not. Hell, for all we know, the Minister of Defence or one of his close aids might be the leak. We just don't know."

"So who can we trust, Mason?"

I studied her face a moment. "I trust you."

"Yeah, me too," she said ambiguously. "So we tell nobody—*no-body*—about the arrangement we've made with Sunny."

"We'll have to tell Nero."

She thought about that. "I trust Nero," she said eventually. "But we call him on a secure line from the Israeli embassy." She looked at me, and there was a fierce intensity in her eyes. "These are crazy times, Mason. All the old certainties are gone. You don't know who you can trust, or who is your enemy."

We drove on in silence and eventually came to Hyde Park. We skirted it and moved down Bayswater Road toward Notting Hill. That was when she said, "And, Mason, next time you make a pass at me, don't do it when I'm about to shoot somebody."

"Make a pass at you? *Next time?*"

She screwed up her face. "Come on! It was so transparent!"

"I was saving your life!"

"Seriously? You think I didn't have him lined up already? Hey!" She looked at me, repressing a laugh. "I get it. Midlife crisis, stress, adrenaline, I'm a desirable woman, you are not sure if you're performing the way you did ten years ago... I get it. Just don't do it if I'm about to shoot some guy."

"But if you're *not* about to shoot some guy...?"

"I've been turning it over. They knew we were there, but did they know *why* we were there? You think they were going to kill us and then go after Sunny? Did they know *he* was there? Have they sent another team after him?"

I sighed quietly to myself.

"They haven't got unlimited resources. There were eight of them. They didn't delegate two to us and two to Sunny. We were their target. Besides, I get the impression Sunny can take care of himself."

"I guess."

"If we tried to find him to protect him, most probably we would draw them to him. There is a chance they don't know he's talking to us. The only people we told were your dad and Sir Lacklan."

"So how did they know we were going to be here?"

"Maybe they've been following us." I smiled and said with more feeling than I intended, "You are hard to miss and easy to follow." She arched an eyebrow at me. I said, "Burgundy S-Type. It's a very beautiful car, and not all that common."

We crossed Notting Hill Gate and cruised down Holland Park Avenue to Holland Road. Shortly after that, she pulled up outside her house. She killed the engine and climbed out. Right to the point where she put the key in the door and opened it, she was smiling a private smile.

At least, I like to think she was.

TEN

"HI, DADDY."

She was standing at the freezer looking in at a stack of pizzas. She looked at me over her shoulder and pointed at the stack, then moved aside, speaking into her cell.

"This is really important, and I need you to listen very, *very* carefully... Yes, I know you do, but even more than usual. We went to meet somebody, and we were followed. There were four of them, and they attacked us..." She took a deep breath and got in my way at the fridge to pull out a couple of bottles of beer. She showed them to me and made a question with her face. I nodded. She kept talking. "Yes, Daddy, I took care of two of them, and Mason took care of the other two. He killed one of them and the other won't be having babies. Yes, I killed both of mine. Daddy, I need you to listen."

She opened a drawer, pulled out an opener, and handed it to me, and pointed to a cupboard where there were glasses.

"The important thing is that we were followed. The only

people who knew we were going were you, Sir Lacklan, and the wife of the man we were going to meet."

I was turning on the oven and felt a tap on my shoulder. I turned, and she made the universal gesture of 'drink' and pointed at the bottles.

"I don't know, Dad"—repeat of gesture for drink—"I know you're not a leak. That makes no sense. I am pretty sure Sir Lacklan isn't, and I am damn sure Mavis isn't—yeah, his wife—but like Mason said, we don't know who Sir Lacklan is talking to. There may be a leak going down the line, right? So this is what I am trying to tell you, if you'd stop interrupting." She took the beer from my hand, and I put the pizzas in the oven. "What comes next has to stay between you and me and Mason."

As I poured my own beer, she put her phone on speaker and set it on the countertop. Gabriel was saying, "What comes next, Aila? I have to be very careful to preserve good relations with the Five Eyes, especially at the moment."

"I know. But listen. Tomorrow we pick up the man they called Sunny and we take him straight to the Israeli Embassy. He brings with him all the evidence Putin is threatening to bring against the UK. We keep him there safe until Nero can take him to the States and give him a change of identity."

He was quiet for a moment, then said, "Okay. This is need to know. The guards on the gate will expect you at what time?"

"As from ten after eleven. All they need to know is a Land Rover is coming in at that time. It's urgent and they don't piss about."

"Okay, what Land Rover?"

"That's the other thing. I need an armored Land Rover

that looks like any old beaten-up Defender from when the UK still had some industry. I know you have one."

"I'll have Dave park it outside your house tonight. He'll put the keys through your letter box."

"You're the best, Daddy."

"Alex, are you there?"

"I'm here."

"Look after her. You're a good man. She's a good woman. She would be good for you. It's a shame you're not a Jew. You're a mensch. Take care of her."

I smiled at her. She smiled and turned away. I said, "I'll take care of her for you, Gabriel. Don't worry."

He muttered something in a sing-song that went like, "For me? Why for me? For you! *For you!*"

She hung up, and we stared at each other a moment, drinking beer. I spoke first.

"Leave here ten-thirty, pick Sunny up at eleven, out onto Ladbroke Grove, and head for Notting Hill gate, Church Street down to High Street Kensington and duck into the embassy at the Kensington Palace Gardens."

"Mm-hmm. Then, and only then, do you call Nero and make arrangements for Sunny's transfer to the United States."

"Agreed. What about the evidence? Technically we should hand it over to the British, but I don't want to do that until they catch their mole."

She stared at the oven and grunted. "How long? I'm hungry."

"Five more minutes. I have to tell Nero and let him decide how we do it. This is a jurisdictional nightmare, and at least he and Sir Lacklan belong to the same organization."

"I said then and only then—"

And I agreed with you. If it was just Sunny that we had to deal with, there would be no question. But it's not. It's the packages of evidence. Nero has to take responsibility for this and decide what to do. He needs to talk to Gabriel and Sir Lacklan. He'll know how to deal with it."

"Because he's a genius."

"That too."

I called him. He answered with his mouth full, and I wondered what time it was in DC.

"Umph?"

"We collect Sunny tomorrow morning. We're going to take him to the Israeli Embassy because we know there is a mole in the British system. Sunny is bringing two packages of evidence with him, the one collected by Nepel and the one collected by Rashid. I need to know what we do with them. Technically they belong to the Brits, but if we hand them over before they find their mole, it could be disastrous."

I put it on speaker, as Gallin had done minutes earlier.

He said, "Understood. I'll talk to Gabriel. You'll have two cars ready at the embassy. You dismount from your vehicle, and Gabriel will take charge of the prisoner. You each take a car, and you each take a disparate route to the City. Aila will go to St Paul's Cathedral, and there she will meet with a man who will approach her. Captain, are you listening?"

"I am."

"The man will identify himself as...err...Snodgrass. He will give you a folded Daily Telegraph, and you will give him something, anything, in a plastic groceries bag. You will each go your separate ways. You return home."

"Alex, you will go to the Bank of Finance and Investment on Threadneedle Street. There you will take a safety deposit box and place the two packages there. From there, you will return to Captain Gallin's house and await instructions. Is that perfectly understood?"

Gallin said, "Perfectly." I said, "Yup."

He said, "I am now going to speak with Gabriel and Sir Lacklan. Only you and I will know of the exact instructions which you will follow. If you don't hear from me, take them as confirmed."

He hung up.

Gallin started pulling the pizzas out of the oven. I said, "The plan makes sense."

"It's good."

"Don't forget your grocery bag of dirty laundry tomorrow."

She started cutting the pizzas with a little more vigor than you'd think necessary. She said, "I guess that's so if anyone is following us, they won't know which one of us..." She trailed off, then said, "You want to watch a movie?"

"Sure. What do you have in mind?"

She shrugged and handed me my pizza. "You want another beer?" She pulled two more beers from the fridge, stuck the opener in her back pocket, and made for the door. "So we don't need to get up for anything. Jeez, I'm pooped." I followed her into the living room, frowning. There she pulled over a couple of small tables for us and settled on the sofa. "Did you ever watch *The Princess Bride*?"

I settled beside her and repressed a laugh. "*The Princess*

what? No. Is it one of those romantic comedies? It doesn't sound like—"

"You'll love it. I've watched it six times, and I want to watch it again. Just relax, nestle down. It's not what you expect."

"Nestle down...?" I picked up a piece of pizza and bit into it.

Forty-five minutes later, as I was consumed with anxiety over whether the Spanish hidalgo Inigo Montoya would die and whether our hero Westley would be paralyzed for life, Gallin snored softly, curled up against my shoulder.

ELEVEN

PORTOBELLO ROAD IS A STREET MARKET IN Notting Hill that runs for about a mile from Pembridge Road in Notting Hill Gate to Layla's Café on the corner of Bonchurch Road, a stone's throw from the Grand Union Canal. Every Friday and Saturday, come rain or shine, it gets packed with thousands of visitors from all over the globe and spills over into side streets, alleys, squares, and gardens.

This particular Saturday, the sun was shining and the streets were jammed with people in plastic flip-flops, shorts, T-shirts, stupid little backpacks, and little plastic bottles of water. As we crawled through the crowds with Gallin at the wheel of her S-Type, she gestured at them with an open hand.

"You want to explain this to me, Mason? This uniform? The uniform of the inclusive? You know what this means? This stupid rucksack and the little bottle of water?"

"Oh, God."

"Come on!" She said that and slapped me in the chest

with the back of her hand. "Are you telling me you don't look at these limp, invertebrate people and fear for the future of our species?"

"Maybe a little," I admitted.

"Wool," she said.

"What, now?"

"Wool. As wool is the uniform of the bleating sheep, who shamble obediently to the slaughter house, so the flip-flops, the little rucksack, and the bottle of water—saturated by the way with pseudo-estrogens—are the uniform of the mindless drones who obey the dictates of the hive of social media." Then she repeated, as though she had not said enough, 'The Hive of Social Media,'" emphasizing the capitalized initial letters. You could tell she had capitalized them by the deliberate tone of her voice.

"Did anybody ever tell you you are very intense, Gallin?"

We were crawling down Chesterton Road toward the top end of the market. She said, "Yeah, you know what I told them?"

"I know you're going to—"

"What is the *point*—"

"Right."

"Of being *alive*—"

"Uh-huh."

"If you are not *intensely* alive? Do you know? Because I don't! We turn right here, Bevington Road."

"He said Blagrobe."

"Bevington runs into Blagrove. Did you like the movie?"

"Yeah, you fell asleep."

"You have a comfortable shoulder that induces sleep. See that tramp? I bet that's him."

We had reached the corner of Raddington Road and Blagrove. The place was milling with people, but there was one guy sitting on the sidewalk with a bottle of Strongbow cider in his hand and a woolen hat pulled down over his ears. A thick beard covered most of the rest of his face, and he had an old canvas bag hanging around his neck and one shoulder.

We pulled over to the side of the road, and the guy struggled to his feet like he was drunk. Gallin unlocked the doors. I was looking everywhere except at the guy with the beard. I wasn't sure it was Sunny, but if it was, I wanted to be aware of anyone approaching him. I couldn't see anyone. All I could see was a mass of milling people going in all directions, some stopping staring at stalls, others in small groups talking. No one stood out. No one looked threatening. No one looked Russian, and nobody looked like a trained killer.

But then usually trained killers don't.

The guy stumbled and leaned on the plane tree on the corner. He leaned over and vomited, then wiped his mouth on his sleeve. Thirty yards away across the road, a guy in a mesh-sleeve shirt pulled his cell from his pocket and spoke into it. He turned to look at the tramp. I said, "There."

Gallin said, "I see him."

I slipped my Sig from my pocket. The tramp went to walk behind the Land Rover, and I thought maybe it wasn't Sunny after all. The guy with the cell put his phone in his pocket and began an easy jog in our direction. At the same time, I saw two other guys turn from what they were doing and start a run toward the rear of the truck. I swore violently under my breath. In the wing mirror, I saw the tramp stumble against the side of the car. Then he had the door open and he was jumping in, screaming, *"Go! Go! Go!"* Gallin floored the gas, and we fishtailed into Raddington Road.

I could hear violent screaming behind me. I craned around my seat and saw Sunny clinging to Gallin's headrest and lashing out with his right foot. The door was still open, and the guy with the mesh sleeve shirt was half inside, clinging to my headrest with one hand and fighting off Sunny's foot with his other, while trying to get a hold of the canvas bag he had around his neck.

I tried to get a bead on the guy, but the way Gallin was swerving, the risk of hitting Sunny was too great. I bellowed, *"Brake!"*

She stood on the brake. The tires screamed. Sunny and the shirt slammed into the back of our seats. I got my bead. As I squeezed the trigger, I saw the blade in his hand. He lunged and cut, and I fired. His face contracted in a horrible grimace. For a moment, his neck went crimson, with all the tendons stretched, but his face was pasty and white. His eyes locked on mine. He half-stood and stumbled back, gripping Sunny's bag. I grabbed the other end, wound it around my wrist, and bellowed, *"Hit the gas!"*

She floored the pedal, and the shirt fell back and rolled out of the open door. We hurtled down Oxford Gardens, screeched, and fishtailed left into Ladbroke Grove. I felt a hand on my shoulder. I gripped it and turned. Sunny's face was a few inches from mine. "Brussels," he said. "The Hague…"

In that instant of chaos, his words made little sense. We had skidded onto the Grove and were hurtling south, down the hill, honking and weaving in and out of traffic. Cars honked back and swerved out of the way. We avoided collisions a dozen times by pure miracle. I glanced at Sunny. He looked bad. He breathed, "Benelux..."I frowned and snapped, "*What?*"

I unwound the bag from my wrist and glanced at Gallin's face. It was impassive. Her eyes were glued to the road ahead as her hands spun the wheel this way and that.

Ahead I saw Ladbroke Grove underground station and the Metropolitan Line overpass forming a bridge over the road. We thundered toward it. Beyond, I could see the intersection with Lancaster Road and beyond that the library on the left. The horn was blaring. People were scattering. We jumped the red lights, and the shadow beneath the overpass engulfed us and flashed by. Then the SUV pulled out of Lancaster road across our path. For a couple of seconds that felt like an eternity, the whole world was the scream of the Land Rover's brakes. Gallin spun the wheel to the right to cut around the SUV's hood, but the Land Rover's rear end kept moving forward and smashed into the side of the SUV with a horrible crunch and screech of tortured metal.

The truck had stalled. It was no more than a second or two before she tried to fire it up again. In that time, a guy in black with a balaclava over his head had stepped around the hood of the SUV. He had a semi-automatic pointed straight at Gallin. At the same time in my peripheral vision, I saw three guys dressed the same way run around the rear end, headed for the side of the Land Rover.

I reacted by instinct without thinking. I shot the guy with the gun, and as I did it I shouted, "*Sunny! Are you okay?*"

The engine choked and coughed. Gallin swore quietly.

There were two guys yanking at the back door. I reached over my shoulder and fired blind. Another shot rang from outside. The engine roared. The back door was wrenched open. I shouted at Gallin, "*Wait!*" and shoved my door open, swinging around as I jumped out. In a fraction of a second, I took in one guy on the blacktop with his head in a pool of blood. Another guy was behind the door leaning in to the back seat. A third was pointing a Glock at my head.

I dropped to one knee and pumped two 9 mm slugs where no man should ever be shot. I stood and aimed through the glass. As I did so, the guy turned and ran. He had Sunny's bag in his hand. I went after him at a sprint, ignoring the blaring traffic and the shouting voices. He'd gone fifteen yards into Lancaster Road and I was closing on him fast when a 1,000 CC Suzuki roared off the sidewalk and skidded between me and him. The rider was waving what looked like an Uzi at me. I braced myself for the impact, took aim as the guy with the bag leapt on the back, and fired as they roared away.

I could hear a lot of shouting behind me and the growl of the damaged Land Rover approaching. In the distance, I could hear a siren wailing. Gallin pulled up beside me, and the door swung open.

"Get in before the mob lynches us," she said. As I swung in, she added, "Sunny is dead. He was knifed by the first guy you shot."

Instinctively I looked in the back seat. It was covered in blood, but there was no sign of Sunny. "Where is he?"

"I dumped him at the crossroads. Call Sir Lacklan and tell him to call off the dogs."

I stared at her a moment, then pulled out my cell.

"Yes?"

"Sir Lacklan. We were ambushed on Ladbroke Grove. Sunny was killed. They took the packages. We need you to call off the cops. They are coming after us."

Gallin spoke loud enough for him to hear her. "We'll make our own way back."

I repeated, "We'll make—"

"I heard. I want a full report."

I snarled, suddenly mad. "Yeah, me too."

I hung up and called Nero. Beside me, I could hear Gallin on her phone. She spoke briefly in Hebrew, then hung up and began to describe figures of eight, weaving among the streets. Nero's voice growled in my ear, "Can't I have breakfast in peace?"

"No. We were ambushed on Ladbroke Grove. Sunny is dead, and both packages were taken. They knew we were coming. They were at the extraction point, and they had a team ready to cut us off on Ladbroke Grove. An SUV and a bike for a quick getaway. They had balaclavas, and they were all dressed the same."

"Dump the vehicle. Go to the Israeli embassy. I am on my way to London. I will break my fast on the plane."

"Oh, good."

I hung up as Gallin pulled up beside a park with a kids' playground inside it. We climbed out, and far in the distance, we could hear sirens. Gallin slammed the door and talked to me across the hood. "I have a car meeting us up on Ledbury Road, outside the Ottolenghi."

We walked a hundred yards up Colville Terrace. She had her arm through mine like we were a strolling couple. We turned right into Ledbury Road and walked another hundred and thirty yards. All the while she was talking to me. Sometimes she laughed and squeezed my arm. I didn't hear a word she was saying. All I could think was that I had let that bag get away, and now our closest ally was going to get dragged into a war with Russia and Iran because I had failed.

Suddenly she was laughing and waving. A Jaguar saloon pulled up beside us, and a handsome guy in shades was grinning up at Gallin.

"Hey, beautiful, imagine seeing you here."

"Give us a ride?"

"How could I say no?"

"You couldn't!"

They both laughed, and we climbed in the back. It was a surreal moment. They didn't talk again. He did a U-turn, and we moved swiftly toward Kensington. I looked at Gallin.

"One second," I said. "It was a matter of one second. If I'd shot the guy taking the bag first."

"No." She shook her head. "Think it through. The other guy would have shot you, and he would have taken the bag. Your judgment was correct. Your order of execution was correct. What you did was damage them and save our lives. Now we go after them." She patted my thigh and squeezed it. "You did good. You'll feel better after lunch."

I frowned, a little confused. "Right."

TWELVE

"Nero is on his way." Gabriel said this as he lowered himself into his chair behind his desk. "But it will be another six hours at least before he is here." He sighed heavily through his nose. "Of course CID cannot talk to us directly, even if they wanted to. Any intelligence we get from them must come through MI5 or ODIN. As far as the SIS is concerned, all the doors have been firmly closed while they make their internal inquiries."

His next sigh somehow managed to communicate that he was not done and we should keep quiet. After a moment, he went on.

"The police took the Land Rover, which was then taken by MI5 who are, as I understand it, scouring it for forensic evidence. Sir Lacklan is with them now, and he will then have to decide how much of what they tell him he can tell me. We are not full members of the Five Eyes." He gestured at me with an open hand. "I would imagine he and/or Nero will brief you appropriately." He turned to Gallin. "I took the liberty of having them bring in your Jaguar to have a look at it. It's downstairs. I don't know if they have found anything."

Gallin raised her eyebrows high. Before she could answer, I said, "Sunny said something before he died."

Gabriel leaned back in his chair. "What did he say?"

"We were doing sixty in a crowded street with people trying to shoot us, so it didn't make a lot of sense right then—"

"What did he say?"

"He said, 'Brussels,' and then 'the Hague.' Now I am guessing he was trying to tell me where they were going to take the packages."

He nodded once. It was more a show of resignation than agreement. "Presumably they will hand it over to their Russian lawyers there so that they can bring their action against the SIS and the UK."

Gallin said, "They've silenced Sunny. We have to recover those packages."

Gabriel raised an eyebrow at his daughter. "How?"

She raised her thumb as 'number one.' "We have to go to Brussels to be on the ground as soon as intelligence is available."

I nodded, and Gabriel said, "Agreed."

She raised her index finger. "Two, we need all eyes on ports, Channel, and airports." She looked at me. "ODIN can help here. We need all available Five Eyes technology scanning every damn person who gets on a plane, a train or a boat, putting them through face recognition and tracking them once they arrive on the other side of the Channel. And three"—she raised her middle finger—"we need all available hands ready to snatch anyone the software recognizes."

He grunted. "It's worth a try."

I stood and moved over by the window to call Nero. Behind me, I heard Gallin saying, "But, Dad, I am beginning to have a real problem with Sir Lacklan. That was one mother of a leak…"

As the phone rang, I heard Gabriel saying, "But Sir Lacklan. I have known him years…"

Nero's voice spoke in my ear. "Alex, I am in the air. Report."

"We're talking with Gabriel."

"Good. And?"

"It's a tall order, but sir, you are going to have to get all available Five Eyes technology focused on airports, Channel Tunnel, and ferry services from the UK to Brussels and the Hague—yesterday! The packages are on their way either to Holland or the Benelux countries, and we need them intercepted on the crossing. Gallin and I are on our way to Brussels."

"Good. You have spoken with Sir Lacklan?"

"No."

"Why not?"

"Because we have sprung a big leak, and we don't know where it is."

He was quiet for a long moment, then said, "All right. Don't wait for me. If necessary, I will go to Brussels or the Hague. Otherwise I'll be in London. Go, get the next flight. I'll make the arrangements for checking travelers in and out of Benelux and the Hague."

"Yes, sir. Thank you."

I hung up and turned. They were both watching me. I raised the phone a couple of inches. "Nero. He's on his way. He'll see to the border surveillance using the Five Eyes technology. He wants us to go immediately to Brussels."

Gabriel nodded. "Go—" The internal phone cut him short. He snatched it up. "Yes."

He listened a moment, then raised his eyes to look at his daughter. "All right. Thank you."

He hung up. "Your car was bugged. It follows logically that your house is being watched and the Land Rover was bugged too, after it was delivered."

"Shit, but it doesn't explain—"

"It does." I cut her short. "To some extent at least. It doesn't explain the leak. The leak goes back before Ukraine. For my money, the leak is a sleeper who was planted here by Colonel Vitsin years ago and has recently been activated. And as soon as they knew that we were being sent to interrogate the prisoners in Ukraine, she would have organized surveillance to keep track of our movements. It's a short step from there to knowing that we would be looking for the evidence. When Sunny took it, they would have been all over us like a rash to see if he was going to try and give it to us. It doesn't tell us who the leak is, though the suspect pool is pretty small, but it does explain how they were on us so fast today."

Gabriel cleared his throat. "I am going to send a couple up to RAF Brize Norton in your Jaguar. Then we are going to smuggle you out in a laundry van that will take you to a friendly hotel, where you will pick up a suitable vehicle that you can drive to the Manor House in Suffolk. There will be a diplomatic helicopter waiting for you there. It will take you to Brussels. There will be a car there for you." He arched an eyebrow at Gallin. "A normal car, like the ones normal people drive. I will book you in at the Hotel Amigo, on Rue de L'Amigo, by the Grand Place in the old town. You will be able to take your weapons through in the diplomatic bag."

He stood and gave his daughter a sudden and fierce embrace. She returned it in the same terms. For a moment, they stood holding each other, then he stared into her eyes, which were spilling tears onto her cheeks.

"Be safe," he said. "Come back, and make your country and your people proud."

She gave a brief nod. "I will.'

He slapped me on the shoulder, sat behind his desk, and we left without another word.

AN HOUR LATER, after changing our clothes and getting together some basic luggage, we were placed into the back of a laundry van that took us to the London Marriott Hotel on Park Lane. There it backed into the service entrance on North Row, and we were bundled out, past slightly bemused staff, down to the parking garage, where we were taken by a guy in a suit who did not speak to a classic TVR Cerbera V8 from 1996: four hundred and forty horses, zero to sixty in three and a half seconds, and a top speed of one hundred and ninety-three miles per hour. And that was in 1996.

Gallin was smiling, but I whipped the keys from the silent man in the suit and thanked him with a nod, a smile, and a wink.

"My turn," I told Gallin. "Last time you drove, we crashed."

It was a two and a half hour drive from the Marriott to the hamlet of Knodishall, near the east coast of England. And once we'd left the M25 freeway and hit the A12 road through the countryside, past Colchester and Ipswich, it was a pleasant drive. We kept our eyes peeled, and I drove with one eye on the rearview, but there was no sign that we had been followed. It looked like Gabriel's ruse had worked.

A little after the village of Farnham, we turned off the A12 and wound our way along twisting, narrow lanes through dappled woodland and farmland until quite suddenly we came to a clearing where the narrow road split into two paths, one bearing right and the other left. In the angle they made, there was a tall gray and black flint wall over which sycamore trees rose and swayed in the afternoon breeze.

Gallin pointed left. "Down there." I followed the track, and we came to a big gate. She pulled out a remote from her jacket, the gate swung open, and we pulled into a large, gravel courtyard.

The house was old and built on a horseshoe design, where the middle wing was the house, and the two side wings were barns, garages, and stables. I pulled up outside the garage, and she looked at me a moment with a funny smile on her face.

"Home," she said. "You know me as English and Israeli. But there is a whole other side to me you don't know."

"Oh God, you mean there's more?"

"My mother's side. Directly, and indirectly, this house goes back to the Danes, before Christianity arrived in

Britain. My mother's family goes back in this area just as long, and at the time of the Norman conquest, her ancestors took possession of this house. It has been in our family, on and off, for a thousand years."

I looked at the ancient, flint building and tried to conceive a thousand years. She grinned at me. "There is a bit of Viking in me."

I laughed. "No kidding. I would never have guessed."

We put the car in the garage and went through a door that had probably been there when Henry VIII was giving the Pope a hard time and into a huge, high-ceilinged hall with oak paneled walls and leaded windows. There was a fireplace you could probably fit a whole Japanese family in and a mahogany staircase that rose to a galleried landing where for a moment I could swear I saw ghosts playing lutes.

I stopped and stood, a little awed, thinking of the thousand years of history I was standing in, but Gallin grabbed my arm and pointed to the tall, gabled windows. "See the lawn, Mr. Mason? That blue and white thing at the end of it is a helicopter. We have to go."

"This place is amazing, Gallin." I took a couple of steps. "You never told me about this."

"Yeah, well, I was waiting for the right time. Come on!"

I followed her to another huge, ancient door. She pushed it open, and as I stepped through, she said, "If we can stop history from happening this week, Mason, maybe this will be here for another thousand years."

I paused, looking down into her beautiful, passionate face and said suddenly, without thinking, "Maybe our kids will live here."

She frowned hard at me and gave me a thump on my arm. It hurt. "Asshole!"

I followed her across the law rubbing my shoulder and wishing there was some way to understand women. Even Freud had given up, though. He had called them the 'Dark Continent.' So I figured it was something of a forlorn hope.

It was a little under an hour's flight from the Knodishall in Suffolk to Brussels International airport. I watched Gallin as she stared at the ancient house shrinking beneath and behind us as we climbed into the air and began to skim over the sprawling woodlands, gradually gaining height.

"Children," she said quietly. Then she turned to me, smiled, and touched my arm. "Sorry, big guy. It's just we are warriors. We don't get to have kids and families and play Scrabble and Cluedo beside the fire. That's for the people we protect, not for us."

I wanted to come back with some wiseass reply, but I couldn't. Every smartass word I reached for died in my throat.

By the time we had landed at the airport and made it to the hotel, dusk was gathering into evening. I stretched out on the bed, and Gallin opened her case and started slamming things. Anything, from her clothes to her toiletries pack, hairbrush, and makeup, she would pick it up, mutter and slam it down again.

"I have nothing!" she said, and then with more emphasis, "*Nothing!*"

I closed my eyes and shook my head. "Can nothing be said actually to exist, Gallin? Isn't nothing really just something that has no meaning for us?"

Her answer came from the bathroom with that marble, tiled echo. It was obscene and not printable. It was followed by, "I'm going down to the chemist," and the slamming of the door.

It was some ten minutes after that that there was a knock at the door. When I opened it, there were two men there. The closest one was about six-two. He was lean and Black with very short hair and a well-cut, pale blue suit.

The man behind him and slightly to his right was three inches shorter with big shoulders, an aquiline nose, and a poorly cut, beige linen suit with no tie.

The Black guy spoke with a resonant French accent.

"Mr. Mason?"

"Who's asking?"

He somehow managed to shrug, spread his hands, and reach for his badge all at the same time. "You ask the question, but the question is like '*yes*' so we can simply say yes, no?"

He showed me his badge and his pal's badge and said, 'I am Field Operative Amin Kateb. This is Field Operative Robert Navarre, of Europol."

I handed the badges back. "Yes, I am Alex Mason, how can I help you gentlemen?"

"We have some questions, Mr. Mason. Can we enter, please?"

"Of course." I stepped aside and waved them in. "This is not a convenient time. We have just arrived, and we are rather tired, but we are always willing to assist the police."

He moved through to the sitting area and put his hands behind his back. "You are not alone." It wasn't so much a question as a statement that invited an answer.

I smiled. "My girlfriend. She's gone out to buy some essentials. Will you sit? Can I order you something—tea, coffee...?"

They both sat on the sofa, side by side. Kateb said, "Mr. Mason, what is your purpose in visiting Belgium?"

I aimed for the urbane in my smile. "Beside the beer and the thrill of visiting the place where Napoleon was finally crushed by the Iron Duke? Just pleasure, Operative Kateb."

I sat in an armchair. He said, "You came by helicopter." He actually said, 'elicopter,' but he meant helicopter.

I allowed my smile to become somewhat dead. "Are you telling me or asking me?"

"It is an unusual way to travel."

"Does doing something unusual come under the jurisdiction of Europol now, Operative Kateb?"

His large, somewhat yellow eyes became hooded. "We live in troubled times, Mr. Mason. It is our job to be vigilant."

I leaned forward with my elbows on my knees. "Then you should be aware of this, Operative Kateb, that the helicopter we arrived in belongs to the Israeli Embassy and is frequently used to transport diplomats and their assistants from London to Brussels. Not so unusual after all. I do hope these inquiries of yours, Operative Kateb, are not motivated by the growing anti-Zionist feelings in Europe."

He took a long time to answer. He just watched me, like he was imagining all the unpleasant things he'd like to do to me. Finally he blinked and looked away.

"No, Mr. Mason. No anti-Zionism. Also no Islamophobia."

"Right, we are all inclusive here. Was there anything else?"

"You are Jewish, Mr. Mason?"

"How is that any of the European Union's business, Operative Kateb?"

"You arrived in an Israeli diplomatic helicopter."

"I'll tell you what, Field Operative Amin Kateb, you find me the European Directive where it says that Israeli diplomatic vehicles can only transport Jews into and out of the Union, and I will tell you whether I am Jewish. Was there anything else?"

He smiled like he was a real nice guy and I had gotten him all wrong. "We are simply concerned for your safety, Mr. Mason. These are troubled, dangerous times. We just want you to know we are looking out for you."

"Well, that's really nice of you, we really appreciate it. I'm sure we'll be just fine."

"How long do you think you'll be here?"

"I don't know. I might like it so much I'll stay and raise a Eurofamily." His face said he didn't think that was funny, so I added, "*Now* was there anything else?"

He stood. I stood with him, and so did the silent wonder, Field Operative Robert Navarre. It was he who spoke now. His voice wasn't so resonant but had the harsh tones of the Pyrenees.

"Are you looking for somebody while you are here, Mr. Mason?"

"Yeah. I am looking for my true self. If you see me, tell me where I am, will you?"

He nodded and smiled. "Is funny." He twisted his hand like he was screwing in a light bulb. "A paradox. Have a peaceful stay in Brussels. If you are need anything"—he pulled a card from his wallet and handed it to me—"you call."

I took the card. "Thanks, I'll be sure to do that."

They left, and fifteen minutes later Gallin came in with a paper bag and stood staring at me.

THIRTEEN

THE BAG SHE WAS HOLDING WAS FULL OF toiletries and cosmetics. She studied my face a moment, then turned and went through the bathroom door and switched on the light.

"Did anyone call?"

"No, not the way you mean it." I went and leaned on the jamb as she took out various pots and tubes and put them on the marble surface. She waved a toothbrush at me.

"You need a new one. What do you mean, not the way I mean it?"

"Two Europol field operatives dropped by, Amin Kateb and Robert-with-a-silent-T Navarre. They wanted us to know they were watching us, they knew we arrived in an Israeli diplomatic chopper, they wanted us to watch our step and to leave as soon as we liked."

She paused in the placing of cosmetics and gave me the once-over. "They didn't ask us to share intelligence or cooperate with them? They just wanted us to leave?"

"Uh-huh."

"That's kind of weird."

"I thought so."

Her cell rang. "Dad." She put it on speaker.

"Is Alex there?"

"Yeah, so am I."

"I can hear you. I don't need to ask. Him I can't hear. Nero is here. He wants to talk to you both."

Nero's voice came on. "I want you to listen with great care to what I am going to say. Not a single person of interest crossed any border from the United Kingdom into Europe in the last seven hours. Now it is barely conceivable that they managed to get the packages out before we set up the Five Eyes monitoring system, but it is extremely unlikely. We will continue monitoring until we reach some kind of resolution. Do you both understand?"

Gallin and I frowned at each other. I said, "Yes..."

"Good. Now you have met George Locke. He is in Brussels at present, STAYING AT THE Dominican, on Leopoldstraat, and he has said he will drop in and share some news with you from his sister."

I rolled my eyes at Gallin and said, "His sis?"

"Yes. Uncle Lacklan is here with me, and he sends his best regards. He says to be careful with those damned foreigners. His words, not mine."

The last bit he said with a total absence of humor.

"We'll do that. And say hi to Uncle Lacklan for us."

"Keep me posted."

He hung up. Gallin and I stared at each other. Finally she said, "What the hell was that all about?" Before I could answer, she went on. "He's talking in code? He never talks in code. And there are no lines more secure than the one they were using. Who does he think is listening in?" I drew breath again, but again she cut across me. "He says, 'Not a single person of interest crossed any border from the United Kingdom into Europe in the last seven hours. Now it is barely conceivable that they managed to get the packages out before we set up the Five Eyes monitoring system, but it is extremely unlikely.' And *then* he starts talking in code? And then he mentions George Locke *by name?*"

"You done?"

"Don't be rude. Yes."

"It was a code within a code."

"Explain."

"He knows everybody thinks he is an eccentric genius. So when he does weird stuff he knows people just dismiss him as that, an eccentric genius who does weird stuff sometimes."

She was watching me with narrowed eyes. "Cut to the chase, cowboy. What's this code within a code stuff?"

I raised my shoulders an eighth of an inch and spread my hands. "Talking as though it was code was to alert me to the fact that he was sending a concealed message."

"Huh, what message?"

"On the face of it that *nobody* had crossed the Channel, and yet George Locke was here. Remember he said we should listen very carefully?"

"Huh." Then she frowned. "On the face of it?"

I nodded. "If you think about it, who was in the room with him? Sir Lacklan and Gabriel. We know that isn't information he would want to conceal from Gabriel. And if it was, he would have spoken to me when you weren't around.

So that leaves Sir Lacklan. But Lacklan has already said he has reservations about Locke, and he himself sends the message, 'Be careful with those foreigners.' So what is Nero actually telling us?"

"That he is concealing information from Sir Lacklan. But what information?"

"That he suspects the leak is Lacklan himself, and not Locke."

"Jesus!"

"On the other hand, if Locke is here, if he has brought the packages, perhaps they are working together."

"Sir Lacklan and George Locke."

"It's conceivable." I gave it a moment's thought, then added, "He mentioned Locke was staying at the Dominican, on Leopoldstraat, and he wanted to share intelligence from SIS." I gave my head a shake. "But what Nero wanted us to understand was that the offer of information from SIS was a delaying tactic so we would wait for him here while he disposed of the packages."

I grabbed my jacket. "Come on, we need to get to the Dominican before he leaves."

She grabbed her jacket and followed me out the door. In the elevator, I said, "You want to wait in the lobby while I go up to his room?"

She nodded. "I run faster than you. No offence. You're fit, you're in shape for a guy your age, but I run faster."

"You think he'll run?"

"You can never be sure. If he does, I'll catch him."

We stepped out of the elevator and made for the desk. There was a guy there talking to the receptionist, who smiled and gestured toward us. George Locke turned, smiled, and spread his arms.

"Well," he said, "if that isn't synchronicity! I was just asking the chap on the desk to call up to you." He took my hand and shook it and gave Gallin a kiss on the cheek. "Alex, Gallin, so nice to see you again and, may I say, in somewhat nicer circumstances. Now I must apologize for the unforgivably short notice, but Commissioner Leo Wolfe has asked me to beg you to dine with him tonight."

We all three stood in silence for a couple of seconds, Gallin frowning, me with narrowed eyes, and Locke smiling politely in a way only the English know how. I broke the silence.

"We were just talking to a friend of yours in London. He said you had some news for us from your sister. We were on our way to your hotel to invite you to dinner so you could tell us all about it."

He laughed like I'd said something really funny.

"Ah, dear old Unc! Yes, well, that is absolutely true. Come along, and I'll drive you over, and we can talk in the car. How's that?"

Gallin looked at me and gave a small shrug. "Sounds good to me. Let's go."

They made to move, and I said, "Leo Wolfe?"

He stopped with his grin frozen on his face. "Do you know him?"

"Austrian, he's the director general for European civil protection and humanitarian aid Operations. It used to be the European Community Humanitarian Aid Office, but then they decided to add the bit about civil protection."

His eyebrows went up. "You are well informed, Mason."

I nodded a few times and stood thinking, looking down at my shoes, trying to bring to mind what Nero had said about that particular directorate general. In the end, I smiled and said, "Sure, let's go eat. I just hope he doesn't serve boiled cabbage and bratwurst."

He had a Mercedes limo waiting outside, and as he opened the rear door to let Gallin in, he laughed. "You have no worries there, old chap. He serves a very fine table."

He opened the other rear door for me. I opened the front passenger door. "I'll ride up front with you," I told him. "That way I can hear you better when you tell us all about sis and Unc."

We climbed in, and he took off down the Rue de Violette. It was narrow and cobbled, though the apartment blocks on either side looked like they belonged more to the '70s than a century where streets were cobbled. But then Brussels is a strange mixture of eighteenth and nineteenth century elegance and *Star Trek: The Next Generation*.

We had gotten as far as the overpass at the Place de la Justice and he still hadn't started talking. I figured it couldn't be more than a ten or fifteen-minute drive, so I asked him.

"You have some information for us? I was told SIS was willing to talk to us."

"About?" He glanced at me, saw the expression on my face, and added, "I mean, in general terms, clearly you are interested in the four chaps who were killed in Ukraine, but what precise information are you after?" He gave a small laugh. "You understand that SIS doesn't volunteer information willy-nilly."

I scowled. "Not even when that willy-nilly information could prevent a war with Russia?"

"What is it you want to know, Mason?"

It was Gallin who answered. "I imagine, Locke, that you know there was a shoot-out between Portobello Market and Ladbroke Grove earlier today."

"I heard something, yes."

"And that a man called Sunny, whom Rashid told us about back in Ukraine, was murdered, and falsified information was taken from him that will allegedly prove that your organization, SIS, engineered the terrorist attack in Moscow. Is any of this news to you?"

He was quiet for a moment with his eyes on the road. As he crossed the Louise Roundabout to join the N24 freeway, he said, "No, Captain, none of that is news to me. So once again I ask you, what, precisely, do you want to know? If I can tell you, I will."

I said, "Did the packages get brought to Brussels or Luxemburg?"

"We can't be absolutely sure, but it seems they may have."

Gallin almost snarled. "They *may* have?"

"Let me finish, Captain. Activity was recorded—and don't ask me to be more precise because I can't be, even if I want to—activity was recorded, and two individuals we have been watching boarded a flight to Amsterdam early this afternoon. These are not people whom we had associated with the Moscow attack. They were followed from the airport, where they hired a car and drove to Brussels. We currently have them under surveillance. But before you cancel your dinner with the commissioner and try to beat the whereabouts of these individuals out of me—yes, Captain, your reputation precedes you—let me tell you that

SIS is aware of the possibility of a leak, and we are liaising with Sir Lacklan, American Central Intelligence, and the Office of the Director of Communication Networks—the Five Eyes. The situation is under control."

He smiled at the mirror and glanced at me as he pulled up outside an apartment block on the corner of Rue du Buisson and the Avenue de General de Gaulle, overlooking a small park taken up almost entirely by a large pond, the Etangs d'Lxelles.

I studied his face for a long moment. "You're not coming up."

"I have work to do. It's the penthouse at number twelve."

"I want to know where those two guys are."

"And I can't tell you yet. Call your boss if you have to and ask him for guidance. I have told you everything I can tell you, and I would strongly advise you to dine with the commissioner." I was about to answer him, but he cut me short. "Let me ask you something, Mason. Did your boss, or yours, Captain, tell you I had information?"

"Yes."

"Right, well I have given you the information I have, and there is no more. So unless you are going to abduct and torture me, I suggest you go and enjoy your dinner with the commissioner."

I got out of the car and slammed the door. Gallin followed suit, and he pulled away and disappeared into the night. A chill breeze was coming off the water and made me shudder. I pulled my cell from my pocket and called Nero.

"Yes."

"He says SIS suspects the packages are held by two guys

who came from London to Brussels via Amsterdam early this afternoon. They are holed up here, and he claims they are being watched by a team including SIS, CIA, Sir Lacklan's men, and ours. He won't give us names or address. He says he can't. But he has brought us to have dinner with Leo Wolfe, the damned commissioner for civil protection and humanitarian aid or something. What do you want us to do?"

"Have dinner."

"*What?*"

"Is your hearing impaired, Alex? I believe you heard me perfectly well. He hosts a splendid table. Enjoy the dinner and the conversation. Report when you return to the hotel."

I hung up. Gallin said, "What did he say?"

I stared at her, shook my head, and made for number twelve.

"'Have dinner,' he said. 'He hosts a splendid table. Enjoy the dinner and the conversation. Report when you return to the hotel.' That's what he said."

Gallin gave a small shrug and came after me.

"Oh," she said. "Okay."

FOURTEEN

Leo Wolfe was a big man. But you got the impression nature had made his body huge in order to accommodate not only his huge personality but the vast ego that went with it.

Leo Wolfe did not open the door to us. He was not the kind of man who opens his own front door. That was something he delegated. He was the kind of man who delegates everything except talking and being adulated. Those were two things he did himself.

The door was opened by a cute girl in a French maid's uniform.

"Mr. Mason and Captain Gallin?"

When she said 'Mr.' she rolled the R in her throat, which made me smile. I said, "Yes, we are here to see Mr. Wolfe."

She gave a little bow and said, "Please, follow me."

We followed the cute swing and bounce of the white bow that secured her apron in place down a long corridor with English hunting prints on the walls, into a vast space that was dining room, drawing room, and library all in one, and out through a huge, sliding glass door to a terrace. There she paused and said prettily, "Monsieur Mason et Capitaine Gallin, monsieur."

She gave us another pretty bow and left, and then the vastness that was Leo Wolfe rose from his chair in an exquisite tuxedo and bowtie and moved toward us like a Spanish galleon in full sail entering a small port. When he spoke, his English was flawless. He might have been a minor English aristocrat. Or a major one.

"Captain Gallin, Mr. Mason, such a pleasure to finally meet you." He took both Gallin's hands in his and led her toward a long table set with a linen cloth, a silver candelabra, and the kinds of glasses, plates, and cutlery that sparkle and sing if you rub them with a wet finger.

"Won't you please sit? And I must apologize for the last-minute invitation."

He deposited Gallin in the chair on his right like a magician setting aside a white bunny he has just produced from his hat and turned to me.

"There are times when events move with merciless speed, and all we can do is adapt as best we can. I hope the meal will make up for any inconvenience caused. Champagne?"

He said this as he sat me on his left and the French maid deposited a large, silver bucket on the table, filled with ice and two bottles of Krug Grand.

The cork popped, the maid poured, and we toasted. As he set down his glass, which he had emptied, he said, "Now, I thought we could open our apetite"—he leaned toward Gallin with an urbane smile—"should it need opening, that is, with a few oysters. They are so fresh they still smell of the ocean. I had them flown in from Dublin just a few hours ago. Then, my dear chap"—this was directed to me—"a smoked Norwegian salmon pate with singed fennel root and fresh mint, followed by an exquisitely tender New York strip steak. The champagne, I think, will go perfectly with the oysters and the salmon. But for the steak I have chosen a one hundred percent Cabernet wine. I know, Mr. Mason, the classic pairing with New York strip is the blend of Cabernet and Sauvignon grapes, but when you taste this wine, you will agree. It is the Château Angélus Hommage à Elisabeth Bouchet, 2019, a Saint Émilion, of course."

I gave him a smile that never made it past my nostrils. "Exactly what I would have chosen."

He leered at me. "Right?" French maid appeared to refill his glass, and he sat back, sipping and watching me. "Never be tied to rules or protocols. What was Rabelais' infamous dictum—"

I either had to interrupt him or shoot him, so I said, "Do as though wilt shall be all of the law."

"Exactly."

Gallin cut in. "An interesting approach for a legislator. Commissioners are legislators, aren't they? You do make law."

"Oh, certainly, we make law. If I am honest with you, as I know I can be, the European Union is the latest incarnation of the Roman Empire, and as such is essentially fascist in its structure." He turned to me. "Modern political observers, Mr. Mason, are somewhat blind. They see three principal power blocks: the West, the East, and Islam. And in this view, the West is seen as the supreme power because it has the most advanced technology. That is to say"—he leaned forward and placed his huge hand on my wrist—"it can project its violence to its borders and beyond with least cost and effort." He sat back, gazing smugly toward the sliding glass doors to the terrace. "But this is a wholly inaccurate view."

It turned out his smug gaze was directed to the French maid and her clone who had emerged with three dishes of mussels sitting on beds of ice and spring onions. They deposited them, refilled our glasses, and faded from view. He picked up an oyster, slurped it noisily from the shell, stretched his neck, and swallowed.

Gallin picked up an oyster and asked it, "What exactly is inaccurate about that view?"

He grunted a brief laugh as he sucked on a second oyster. He sipped his champagne to help it down, and with a big happy sigh, he said, "The view of the West is completely inaccurate. Totally out of date. The glimmering mirage of a united, Western democratic beacon for the rest of the world to follow and aspire to, led by fearless Americans brandishing the stars and stripes of hope!" He threw back his head and laughed out loud. "For three, maybe four decades out of fifteen thousand years of history, this illusion held. It started in '47 as the war ended and began its demise ten years later in '57 as the European Economic Community enshrined the Treaty of Rome as its qua-constitution."

Gallin said: "The European Economic Community, the brainchild of the Third Reich."

"Correct. Thus the unelected Commission is the true legislature. But more to the point, my dear Captain, is the fact that there is no 'West.' The West was an illusion created by the existence of NATO. NATO appeared to show us as a united body against the threat of communism. But that was a brief moment, a long time ago."

I shook my head, set a shell down, and sipped my champagne.

"That's not true anymore? I don't follow you. Why is Russia so scared of Ukraine joining NATO? Who shot down the barrage of three hundred drones and missiles Iran fired at Israel..."

But even as I asked it, I began to get a vague glimmer of what he was saying. I could see in Gallin's eyes that she had seen it too. Leo was smiling at me.

"Let me come to Ukraine in a moment. Let us start with Israel. Of course Israel is not part of NATO, though her two biggest allies are members: the UK and the US. And these were the two who assisted Israel in blocking that attack. Note!" He raised his right index finger. "As soon as the attack was blocked, they backed away and distanced themselves. Then Israel, *acting alone*, put a shot across Iran's bows, striking deep inside her territory in spitting distance of an airbase and, most important, a nuclear power plant. This was a warning which Iran heeded." He paused, raised his glass, and gazed a moment at the sparkling wine. "America and the UK. The aircraft carrier UK, positioned off the coast of Europe so that the US can project her violence into Europe if she needs to. The UK is a valuable asset to the US. But make no mistake: The power block is the US, and the UK is an extension of that power."

For a moment, he sat forward, waving his right hand from right to left, like he was waving away smoke. Then he suddenly expostulated, "Completely different! *Completely different* is the European Union. And observe: already President Trump is insinuating strongly that the United States does not need NATO. NATO is a financial drain on the US, who is protected by two oceans and the most advanced technology on the planet."

I asked, "Are you telling me that in your opinion NATO is on its way out?"

Gallin snorted and dropped her last empty shell in the ice. "That's ridiculous. NATO is the greatest concentration of military power on Earth, in history. All of the Western economy depends on it. It's here to stay."

A nasty smile crept up the side of Wolfe's face.

"If there were such a thing as a Western economy, I would agree with you. But what we actually have is a broken, shambling Britain with a senile, crippled political system and a broken military overrun with homosexuals and Muslims, you have a United States of America which is ever more isolationist and will, in a very short time, withdraw from NATO, and then you have a very rich, powerful European Union which is structurally fascist and differs from the US and the UK in only one respect. It has no united army..."

He trailed off, waiting to see if the penny would drop.

It dropped. "So Russia accuses the UK of financing and masterminding an Islamic attack on Moscow, it adduces proof of the UK's involvement in the attack before the International Court of Justice and declares it an act of war..."

Wolfe was nodding. Gallin took over.

"The UK's NATO allies, led no doubt by France and Germany, declare outrage at what the UK has done. The US, seeing the looming threat of a very expensive war with

Russia, finally takes the step and withdraws, the UK either withdraws or is ejected, and the European Union takes possession of what is left of NATO and converts it into its own Euro-Army, essential in an ever more unstable world."

I said, "This is why Macron has been so vocal against Russia in Ukraine. Europe moves in, Russia backs down, and the EU gets Ukraine, the grain basket of Europe."

He threw back his head again and roared with laughter. "These are the little games we discuss with Klaus at the World Economic Forum and at Bilderberg."

Gallin said, "Klaus?"

I'd heard Nero talk about him. I said, "Klaus Schwab. He was the man who persuaded Justin Trudeau to close people's bank accounts if they refused to get the COVID vaccine."

"Oh, nice guy."

We were silent a moment while the cloned maids cleared away our plates and replaced them with the salmon pate. They refilled our glasses and faded into the shadows again.

Leo picked up his knife and a small piece of toast and muttered, "Your very good health!" A moment later, he leaned back in his seat and spoke through a very full mouth, punctuating his words with the sound 'mph.'

"One of the, mph, reasons I was mph keen to have you over, mph, you see was—" He drained his glass and went on. "There is something I should really like you to understand. And it is this." He turned to Gallin. "Captain, do you know what pain is?"

Her eyes narrowed. "I have experienced it, and I have inflicted it."

He was shaking his head. "For millions of years, human

beings were held to the Earth by gravity. They experienced it every day, but they did not—and still do not—know what it is. Do you know what pain is?"

She looked at me and gave a small shrug. Leo went on.

"Pain is contraction." He squeezed his hand into a fist. "Pleasure is relaxation." He opened his hand. He closed and opened his fist again. "Contraction and expansion are the two potentials that are born immediately from three dimensions of space. So! If you have space, pain is an inevitable consequence. Where there are three dimensions of space, there must be pain. And this, my friends, leads to the First Law of Politics."

"And what's that?" I asked.

"Violence is the fundamental basis of all temporal power. The more violence you are capable of inflicting, the more power you have. There is no power without violence. If I can inflict pain—that is violence, right? If I can inflict pain on you, then I can get something from you. The more pain I can inflict, the more I can get from you."

I gave a weary nod and spread salmon pate on my toast. "Your colleague Humberto da Silva explained the same thing to me."

"You killed him."[1]

He said it quite impassively, gazing down at his plate as he loaded another piece of toast.

I glanced at Gallin. She was watching me. I turned my attention to him and arched an eyebrow. "What makes you say that?"

"Is it not true?"

---

1. See Mason 13, *Brotherhood of the Goat*

"You know I couldn't answer that, even if I wanted to. But I can't think of anyone alive, aside from myself, who would know how Humberto da Silva died."

His smile was one of real pleasure. "Captain Gallin was there."

"No, she wasn't."

My mind went back. Gallin had been in another room, where a psychopath had her hair in his left hand and a razor-sharp knife in his right.

Wolfe shrugged. "He was shot fifteen times. He was off his head on some mind-altering drug he was obsessed with, but he didn't shoot himself. You can shoot yourself once, maybe twice, but not fifteen times. You were by your own admission the only person there who could have shot him."

"If that's true, and I am not saying it is, it proved a flaw in his theory. Violence on its own is not enough; it must be supported by intelligence."

"Not a flaw, Mr. Mason, a qualification. Because all intelligence does is wrest the ability to inflict violence from one person to another. The basic ground of the theory is sound. Violence is the source of temporal power."

"Okay, I can't argue with that. Why is it something that you wanted us to understand?"

The smile faded from his face as he spread the last bit of salmon pate on his toast. "Violence," he said, "is not a single thing. It is not a strike, a blow. It can come in many forms, and it has many aspects. For the political animal, for the political *beast* in search of great world power, one element is vital. Mr. Trump has understood this very well. And it is this..."

He stopped and spent a long moment looking at Gallin,

then he turned to me. "You never, never, *never* forgive. You may pardon for political expediency, but you *never* forgive. On the other hand, you *always* seek revenge."

He sat back as the French maids came and removed our plates and brought us New York strip steaks and a bottle of 2019 Saint Émilion. There was also a dish of sautéed potatoes, another of steamed, buttered broccoli, and some Vichy carrots.

Leo Wolfe cut into his steak and watched the warm blood ooze and mix with the oil.

"England betrayed us," he said.

Gallin said, "Brexit."

He nodded. "We had the crown of empire in our hands. Federation and militarization were the next steps. But faithless Albion, she turned away and betrayed us." His face curled with contempt. "The voice of the people!" He spat the words. "It hurt us and weakened us. What we want you, and Sir Lacklan Orme, and the hysterical morons who inhabit Westminster these days, and their friends across the Atlantic... what we want you to understand is that it will not hurt us if Russia breaks Britain. It will weaken the States because it will lose its biggest aircraft carrier. But it will not hurt Europe. On the contrary, we will have our revenge, and we will rise to the dominant position on the globe. We have the technology, we have the industry; all we have lacked until now is the military." He leered at me. "The means to administer violence."

The steak was delicious, and the wine, which I knew from Nero came in at one and a half grand a bottle, was superb. I took some time out to enjoy them, then leaned back in my chair and said, "I understand everything you have said to me, Mr. Wolfe, but I still don't understand why you have felt the need to tell us."

He chuckled. It was a complacent, self-satisfied chuckle.

"Europe is unique," he said suddenly. "We are concerned not only with great military power, but with elegance and culture. Think of it like this: An American will put a gun to your head and say, 'Git outta town, motherfucker, or I'll blow your goddamn head off!' An Englishman of the old school will draw his sword from his cane and tell you, 'You'd better clear off, old chap, or there'll be consequences, what!' A European will demonstrate his power by giving you the best meal and the best wine you are likely to enjoy anywhere in the world and convey to you that the world has changed, and if you cross the line, if you abuse his hospitality, he will...*annihilate* you completely."

FIFTEEN

WE WERE LOOKING AT THE MOON RISING OVER THE ancient skyline of Brussels, sitting on the terrace of our suite sipping a nightcap of twenty-one-year-old Bushmills.

"As ego trips go," Gallin said, "it was certainly one of the most spectacular I have seen."

"You know, they tell you that absolute power corrupts absolutely. What they don't tell you is that it drives you out of your mind." I pointed over the terrace at the buildings and the sparkling city lights and the ceaseless traffic. "All of those eight billion plus people out there, they see their political leaders on the TV, taking their photo ops and striding in and out of magnificent, historic buildings, and they think they are sane, normal people. They don't realize that they are all insane."

Gallin nodded and chinked my glass with hers. "And yet throughout the centuries, it has been demonstrated again and again, emperors who thought they were gods, crazy bastards—in the lifetimes of people we know—who thought it was a good idea to build concentration camps, exterminate an entire race of human beings and—wait for it—use psychics to guide them."

I nodded and chinked her glass. "These were people with college educations from Europe's most civilized country. But it doesn't end there. In the 1980s, these mature, sane grown-up leaders of ours had amassed a total of almost seventy thousand nuclear warheads. Even today, between the Brits and the USA, we have about five thousand five hundred warheads. And we think our political leaders are sane. But most of them are like Leo or worse."

"So you think he was bullshitting us?"

"No, I think he was telling us that if we went after the guys who have the packages, we could wind up spending the next fifteen years in a German prison. And not the sort where they take you to the Caribbean to swim with dolphins. I think they also wanted to send the message in such a way that it would get through to Nero and the brass back home."

She grunted.

"And all the while we were listening to his BS, Locke was probably collecting the evidence and delivering it to the ICJ in the Hague."

"I'm not sure. I don't think Nero would have told us to go and see Wolfe unless he had a reason. And he would not have neglected the packages. There is more to this than we can see, Gallin."

She grunted again. "So what do we do now?"

I thought about it, watching the translucent light of the moon make ancient silhouettes of the city.

"We find out where those guys are, we go, and we collect

the packages." I smiled at Gallin, who was smiling back at me. I added, "And we show Leo and his pals that it is not enough to have access to violence; you have to be sane too."

She chuckled and sipped her whiskey. "Ask Adolph, he'll tell ya." Then she asked the question I was asking myself. "So how do we find out where these guys are?"

I glared at the moon, and she seemed to sneer back.

"We go lateral," I said. "We have been following Muslim moonshine when we should have been looking for Russian…"

She looked into her whiskey. "You can't think of anything that alliterates with Russian, can you?"

"Ruffians. Seriously, Gallin. We have been fixating on those four Muslim guys and a possible English mole. But we have been ignoring what was probably the most important clue we had. And Leo Wolfe all but confirmed it tonight."

"A Russian colonel described as the crazy bitch. Alexandrina Vitsin."

"So when Locke said the guys they were following were not guys they would normally look for in an operation like this, he was telling the truth. The guys who took the packages handed them off to Russians. And the Russians came over to Brussels…" I trailed off as I realized my line of reasoning had suddenly grown weak.

Gallin was there to point it out in case I had missed it. "They didn't come to Brussels. They went to Amsterdam. And instead of driving thirty miles to the Hague, they drove one hundred and ten miles to Brussels." She shrugged with only a hint of smugness. "I'm not saying you're wrong. Well"—she shrugged again—"I am, but—"

I snapped my fingers and pointed at her. "Vitsin!"

"Come again?"

"Colonel Alexandrina Vitsin is in Brussels!"

She was shaking her head, shrugging, and wincing all at the same time. "How could you possibly know... I mean *why?* Why would she...?"

"Commissioner Leo Wolfe just got through telling us. The European Commission would like nothing better than to see the UK broken, a shattered, smoldering example of what happens to you if you defy the might of the Superstate. If in doing that they can hurt the US, so much the better."

She still had her face screwed up.

"Stay with me, Gallin. The US and the UK have one thing in common, and that is a basic belief in free markets and small government. The UK and Russia share a belief in central planning and state control. It's why Brexit happened in the first place. Suddenly, Russia and the EU have become natural—if temporary—allies. Think about it! Think about it! For decades, Interpol, Europol, SIS, MI5, CIA Five Eyes—you name it, we have all been collaborating against Islamic terrorism. And now suddenly an EU commissioner—the director general *for European Civil Protection*—invites us to dinner to warn us off the kind of investigation every damned law enforcement agency in the West is not only conducting but collaborating on. That doesn't make sense. And not only that; he is at pains to stress to us that the EU is no longer part of the West. What is it...?"

"A superstate built on a fascist—or Soviet—model, with central planning and restrictive state control."

"What he did not want us to find, the investigation he was warning us off, was the alliance: the involvement of the

European Union in bringing down the UK, and by a domino effect, harming the US and crippling NATO."

"Sweet Jesus, Mason! Are you serious?"

I flopped back in my chair. "I sure hope not, but it's the only way it makes sense."

"So we are looking for two Russians who crossed from London to Amsterdam..." She was dialing while she spoke. I stood and went inside, took my cell from my jacket, and called Nero.

"You have finished dinner?"

"Yeah, we're back at the hotel."

"What did he tell you?"

"To lay off, the EU is no longer part of the West, and revenge and violence are the basis of power. Oh, and they'd be happy to see the UK sink under the North Sea."

"Did he serve Krug or Bolinger?"

I struggled for a moment, staring at the ceiling.

"Krug, sir. I think we need to be looking for—"

"Oysters?"

"...yes!"

"Fresh or frozen?"

"Fresh! Sir, I think we need to be searching for two Russian agents who crossed from London to Amsterdam yesterday. I believe Colonel Alexandrina Vitsin is behind this, and Russia and the EU are cooperating."

"Yes, it is not clear whether Ursula is moving this or the powers behind her. My own feeling is that this comes from the forces behind the World Economic Forum and Davos."

"You knew..."

"I suspected, Alex. If he had given you Bolinger and

frozen oysters, I would have suspected a red herring. But with Krug and fresh oysters—from Dublin?"

"Yes."

"So he was deadly serious. I know Leo very well."

"Clearly."

"He is quite insane, like most of them. But he is brilliant, and his table is beyond reproach."

"Sir, I need to know where these Russian agents are."

"Locke has them covered, and we have Locke covered. Get some rest. We'll discuss your next move in the morning. I want to see what they do next."

I grunted. "I need to know something. The Russian agents took this stuff to Amsterdam. Why did they not take it to the Hague? Is it because Vitsin is in Brussels?"

He was quiet for a moment, then, "She will want to have sight of it before it is presented to the authorities. And I imagine they will want to put it together with other computer-generated false evidence as a package, probably to be presented by the Russian Ambassador to the European Union."

"Right."

"Get some rest, Alex."

"Thank you, sir, you too."

I walked back to the terrace and stood leaning on the sliding door, looking at Gallin. She had her cell in front of her and was gazing out at the moon, making its domed and steepled silhouettes. I said:

"They have Locke watching them. We are watching Locke. Nero, son of a gun, suspected all of this. He's playing a cool game, but it's a damned risky one."

She turned and looked at me a moment, then nodded.

"We've seen the Russian and EU connection, Mason, but we mustn't forget the Iran-Israel connection. If they pull this off, the whole global balance of power gets turned on its head."

"I know."

"Europe and Russia are the big winners, the US loses some, but not so you'd notice much. The big, big losers are the UK and Israel."

"What did your dad say?"

"He said find the Russian agents, kill them, and destroy the evidence. Is that what Nero said?"

I gave my head a single shake. "No, he said we'd discuss it in the morning. He wants to watch, see what happens, who's involved."

She echoed my shake of the head and looked away at the moon.

"He's a genius, and he is almost never wrong. But he is wrong this time. The stakes are too high."

She looked back at me, and her face was asking if I was going to agree, if I was going to support her. I said, "Come on, let's get some sleep. There's nothing we can do tonight." I hesitated, then frowned. "Did Gabriel tell you where these two agents are holed up?"

"No, Nero wouldn't tell him."

I sighed. "Then for the moment we need to play Nero's game."

"Nero's game." She took a deep breath and released it as a sigh. "Yeah, we'll play Nero's game, for now."

. . .

AT FIVE A.M., an alert on my phone woke me. I got up on one elbow and saw Gallin's silhouette framed against the sliding glass doors. The moonlight outside was still bright. I spoke as I fumbled for my phone.

"You need to rest. Come to bed."

Her silhouette shifted, and her disembodied voice said, "What are you, my husband now?"

I grunted and looked at the message on my cell. It was from Nero.

They are on the move. Meet Locke at 116 Rue Marie Collart, in the Calevoet district. Use your discretion.

I swung out of bed. "Nero. They're on the move. 116 Rue Marie Collart, Calevoet district. We meet Locke there and use our discretion."

I was already dressed and had my jacket on and my Sig holstered by the time I'd finished. Gallin was moving for the door.

It was a twenty-five minute drive from the hotel to the Calevoet suburb. Thanks to the early hour and Gallin's brutal style of driving, we got there in a little under twenty. We approached along Grote Baan, and as we approached the Thai Chine restaurant on the corner of Rue Marie Collart, a figure stepped out of the shadows and approached the edge of the sidewalk. Gallin slowed, and I recognized Locke. I opened the door and got out as she came to a halt.

"What's happening?"

"Good morning to you too. A car arrived about an hour ago."

Gallin was out of the car and approaching. "Where are your men?"

"Mind your own goddamn business, that's where. I've

been ordered to cooperate with you, and that's what I am going to do, under a strictly limited interpretation of that word. But don't run away with the idea that you're taking control of this operation."

Gallin gave a brief nod. "I think I get your gist. Thanks."

He ignored her and turned to me. "About an hour ago, a limo arrived and pulled into the drive. We don't know who they are. We ran the plates, and it's a rental car, rented in Holland by a Mr. Johan Schmitt. Since then, there has been activity in the house, but nothing more."

"An hour ago, and we only hear about this now?"

He took a step closer to me and placed his finger on my chest.

"You listen to me, Mason. I know you and your Mossad pal are out for my blood. I get it, and I am being patient. But when I notified your boss, it had been less than half an hour, and this may come as a shock to you, but I have my job to do, and you are not my top priority. Any other questions?"

"We need to know what's going down in that house."

"We haven't had time to get in there and bug the place. We're doing the best we can from outside. But nobody gets in that street. Not even me. Get in your car and stay out of sight, and radio silence, please. I'll keep you posted."

He crossed the sidewalk and climbed into his own vehicle parked there. We got back in our own car and waited in silence.

Half an hour later, as the horizon was turning gray and sporadic traffic was beginning to appear on the roads, my cell rang. It was Locke. I put it on speaker.

"We're moving. Follow me. Keep your distance." It was a long and winding road. The limo was headed slowly and steadily into town. He had four vehicles tailing him, and I'd be prepared to go ten to one he had no idea. They were pros, and I only knew they were there because I saw them take off after him. He had one in front, two behind, in different lanes, and then there was us tailing Locke.

At one point, one of the cars peeled off and then rejoined the pursuit behind us, closing gradually. Later, the lead car took an exit to the right, and Locke overtook the limo. We followed him, and the tail car closed in. It looked and felt just like normal, early morning traffic, and I'd have been surprised if the driver of the limo noticed a damn thing.

At the intersection of the E19 and the N261, he turned right and east and began to accelerate. We followed but let him pull ahead.

At the Avenue Winston Churchill, he turned right again, and Gallin began to close on him, forcing Locke to fall behind us. The street lamps were still glowing against the dawn sky, but the molten sun was beginning to bulge over the city skyline.

At Chaussée de Waterloo, with the Ravin du Bois de la Cambre park ahead of us, the limo turned left onto Waterloo and then took the next right at Avenue Legrand. Another couple of turns had him on the Avenue Lloyd George. At the end, where Lloyd George meets Franklin Roosevelt, he turned into a parking garage under a very groovy apartment block that looked like it had been constructed two hundred years before the motorcar was invented.

There were parking spaces on the righthand side, in the shade of the trees in the park. Gallin pulled in and killed the engine.

She said, "Why? This is where all the embassies are. Who are they visiting here?"

I jabbed my thumb at the window. "The Russian Embassy is two miles from here, on the Avenue de Fré. But just around the corner to the left, about two or three hundred yards up, is the Russian visa application center. It's like an apartment block eight stories high. I figure they have space in there for more than a few visa applications."

She was staring at me. "What's your point?"

"Vitsin is in Brussels." I pointed across her at the exquisite 17th century building. "That's her apartment, and she has her office around the corner." Gallin stared. I added, "And she just got her hands on the evidence."

"Son of a bitch."

"Who?"

She turned to face me, and her eyes burned into me. "That son of a bitch, Locke!"

I shook my head. "Take it easy, Gallin. He followed Nero's instructions to the letter."

"What the hell do we do now?"

I turned in my seat and watched the other cars pass and disperse. Then I frowned hard at the building, wondering what kind of security it had. If Leo Wolfe had been right, there was no way the Belgian government was going to permit, much less participate in, a raid on a house that was hosting a Russian colonel—probably with diplomatic status.

"Use our discretion," I said.

"My discretion says we go in and take the damned evidence."

"We can't."

"Says who?"

"Says a little thought, Gallin! If we go barging in there shooting everyone, aside from the fact that we will both die, they will blame the Brits again—and their American buddies —this time for trying to steal the evidence. It will just make matters worse. Besides, when I die, I don't want it to be because I was shot by a Belgian."

"So what the hell do we do, Mason? We can't just sit here and let this happen! And where the hell is that son of a bitch Locke?"

"Think," I said in the calmest, most annoying voice I had. "They have to get this stuff from Brussels to the Hague, right?"

"We ambush them on the way."

"Right now I can't think of another way to do it."

"Who the hell needs another way to do it? Let's do it!"

SIXTEEN

WE WAITED TWO HOURS.

During that time, Gallin made a call. Twenty minutes after the call, she got out of the car and hailed a taxi that happened to be passing. The taxi took her away and down the west side of the park, on a trajectory of a little less than two miles. When she returned some fifteen minutes later, it was in an F-Type Jaguar. She pulled in beside our rental, got out, and climbed back behind the wheel. Then she handed me a brown paper bag and said, "Don't mess this up, Mason. You want me to do it?"

"Sure. You do it, if you can give me a good reason why you are a better actor than I am and if you can explain to me why a false moustache would be more convincing on you than on me."

"I dunno." She looked away, out the driver's window and wiggled her fingers around her cheeks. "Bone structure, bearing..."

I fished in the bag and pulled out a fake moustache and a

wig with shaggy gray hair. She said, "He said it was all they had at short notice."

I pulled it on and stuck the moustache on my upper lip. She reached over and gave it a few yanks and twists and muttered, "It's an improvement. You should go for this look."

Then I pulled out a wad of blue gum and handed it to Gallin. She started squashing it and pulling it, while I pulled out a pint of whiskey and started swilling it around my mouth. I may have swallowed some by accident, but the quarter pint I spilled down my shirt was not accidental.

Fifteen minutes later, Gallin handed me the gum and snapped, "Garage door is opening. Go!"

I opened the car door with the bottle of whiskey still in my hand and walked unsteadily across the road while she slipped out and got behind the wheel of the F-Type. When I reached the sidewalk, I turned right and headed toward the apartment block where I had assumed Colonel Vitsin had her apartment. It wasn't easy, but I got the timing about right and reached the drive down to her parking garage just as the Mercedes saloon was coming up. I collided with the front right wing, dropped the bottle of whiskey and let it smash by the front wheel, staggered and fell on the hood, then slipped off onto the road.

The car stopped abruptly, and the front passenger door opened. I peered up and saw a big guy in a blue suit whose head looked like it had been carved out of a giant, peeled potato. His eyes weren't so much windows into his soul as small portholes into not a lot. I waved my left hand at him and shouted drunkenly, "God dammit, you damned frog! You broke my damned whiskey!"

I could tell by his face he was thinking about giving me a good kicking while I lay there. He glanced right and left and decided there was too much traffic and too many witnesses. While he did that, I grabbed a hold of the hood, squashed the blue gum containing the tracking device under his bumper, and struggled to my feet. I stood and swayed a moment, peering through the windshield. I could see the driver. I pointed at him. "You look where you're damn-well goin', you lousy French good for nothin'!"

I squared my shoulders and, as Potato Head climbed back in the car, I walked real slow past the hood, staring down the driver. It gave me a chance to scan the back seat, and I was pretty sure I made out two passengers in the back. One of them could have been a woman. When I was out of their way, I watched them pull out and cross Roosevelt to head up Boulevard General Jacques, otherwise known as R21, which would lead them north, toward the Netherlands.

When they were out of sight, I ran back across the road and climbed in beside Gallin in the F-Type. She already had the engine running and reversed out. On the dash, she had what looked like a large cell with a roadmap, like a SatNav, with a flashing light moving up General Jacques.

"How'd I do?" I said, pulling off the wig and the moustache.

"I dunno, I was distracted by this drunken asshole who almost got himself killed."

"Huh, funny."

"You stink of whiskey." She turned, grinned at me, and gave me a disconcerting wink. "Makes me wanna drink you all up!" Then she threw back her head and laughed.

"You're never happier than when you're hunting some-one, right?"

"Right? Pick a spot, will you?"

I was scanning the road ahead on my cell. I spoke absently, half to myself.

"Okay, nothing is remote here. Remoteness is not a thing in the Benelux countries. But the closest we get to remote is as we leave Wolvertem, it's about nine miles from here as the crow flies, say eleven or twelve by road. It's a very small town. We skirt it on the east and then we have a stretch of about three miles of open fields. That's where we hit them."

"Okay, good. What's the plan?"

I thought about it. Before I could answer, she said, "As we pass Wolvertem, I start to close. As we leave the town, I hit the gas, indicating like I plan to overtake. The driver will see it's a Jag, and he will not want to get into a race. He wants to keep a low profile, and his car is probably bullet-proof anyway, so he is going to let us pass."

"Okay."

"You blow out his tires and I ram him. We blow out the glass. Four shots on the same spot will break it. Kill them and take the evidence."

I nodded. "That's a good plan. What about extraction?"

"You have ten minutes to come up with an extraction plan."

After ten minutes, we were leaving the city by the A12 and heading out into the countryside. I said, "The extraction plan is do the unexpected. Drive back south to Luxemburg and have an ODIN plane meet us there."

"Hundred miles plus in a car that isn't exactly inconspicuous."

"We could get out and walk or catch a bus. But if we take back roads, we can make it in two hours."

"Or we go straight back to the Israeli embassy."

"They'll expect that."

"In Luxemburg. Okay, here we go, closing in."

Ahead of us, the road curved gently to the right, and as we left the town of Wolvertem behind, the road straightened out for about three miles through empty fields. Gallin floored the pedal, hit fifth and sixth with the stick shift, and the Jag surged forward, thundering toward the black limo ahead. She hit the left indicator like she was planning to pass and started honking as the limo swelled in the windshield.

I pulled the Sig from under my arm and, as we drew level, I lowered the window. I yelled at her, "*Overtake! I'm going for the driver first, then the tires if I have to!*"

It had struck me that if you want to shoot through bulletproof glass, the glass approaching the bullet at seventy miles per hour attached to a two-ton car will probably help, so as our trunk came level with their hood, I leaned out the window, got a bead on the driver, and sent six lead slugs his way. The windshield became a dense spider's web, then imploded on the sixth slug. The limo swerved violently and plunged into the ditch beside the road. Gallin screeched to a halt, slammed into reverse, and whined back over the forty feet that separated us.

I already had the door open, and as she stopped, I climbed out and approached the limo with the Sig held out in front of me. I could see the driver through the shattered windshield. He was gaping, and his eyes had rolled up. He had a couple of red holes in his head and one in his chest. I could hear Gallin approaching behind me.

The front passenger door swung open, and Potato Head got out looking as mad as he was confused. He had a gun in his hand, so I put a slug through his head, and his brains erupted over the field. Now there was a corner of Belgium that would be forever Russia.

I glanced at Gallin. "Cover me."

She stayed on the road with her gun trained on the near back door. I slid down the bank and took a hold of the handle. I looked at Gallin. She nodded, and I wrenched open the door. There was a *crack!* Then Gallin's BUL spat four times: one double tap, then another.

I peered around the door as Gallin skidded down the bank. There were two guys, both dead. She'd hit them both in the heart. The nearest one was dressed as a woman in a dark green military uniform with a white wig. The other one was another potato head.

I could feel my heart pounding, near to panic. "It was a feint, a distraction. The evidence isn't even in this damn car! *God dammit!*"

Gallin was already inside the car, tearing at their clothes and pulling out their pockets. I wrenched open the driver's door and opened the trunk, but I knew what I was going to find: nothing.

It was as I pulled my head out of the empty trunk that I heard the speeding engines behind us. Gallin's ass emerged from the rear door, and she stood, glaring at the three approaching vehicles. "There's not a damned thing in there. Vitsin is probably on her way to Russia right now with all the evidence. We are in deep shite, Mason."

"In more ways than one."

I had my cell to my ear. When Nero answered, I said, "Listen don't talk. We have no time. Pursued limo from Vitsin's apartment in Brussels toward Holland. Vitsin apparently aboard. Killed driver and escort outside Wolvertem. It was a decoy. Assume Vitsin en route Moscow with evidence. Belgian cops arriving now at scene of crash. Over."

I hung up and put my cell in my pocket. The two trucks and an Audi sedan pulled up. The trucks had flashing lights, and four cops in paramilitary uniform spilled out. What emerged from the Audi was George Locke. In flawless French, he told the cops to search us and cuff us. While he watched, they took our weapons, our wallets, and our IDs.

"You two." He said it smiling and shaking his head. "Always kind of three steps behind the game, aren't you?" His gaze drifted to the limo. "But this, this is a real mess. Four Russian diplomatic staff." He peered at the guy in drag and chuckled. "I didn't realize the whole transgender thing had reached Moscow, but I suppose we must applaud their progressive thinking." He turned back to Gallin, gave her the once-over, and then looked at me. "But you two, the murder of four diplomatic staff, espionage, no doubt, possession of unlicensed firearms. I'd say you're in a lot of trouble. Somebody should have warned you to behave while you were in Belgium. Oh, wait, somebody did! But you didn't listen, did you?"

He stepped up close to Gallin. "I'm going to enjoy visiting you and interrogating you in prison, Captain Gallin."

He turned to face me. "I saw you on the phone, Mason. Don't build up your hopes. There will be no treaties or conventions to help you. You will not go to prison in Belgium. You are both going first to Kaliningrad, and then to hell."

As if on cue, the sound of a chopper reached us, approaching from Brussels. It settled in the field, about forty yards from us, with the rotors idling. Locke raised his voice over the sound of the chopper. "Let's go for a ride, boys and girls. Let's go visit Auntie Alexandrina."

Four of the paramilitary cops came with us. Two escorted me, and two took Gallin. We clambered over the fence and trudged across the field. A guy I assumed was the copilot got out and slid open the door for us, and we climbed aboard. We got seated and were strapped in, and the chopper thundered and began to rise. Gallin was sitting opposite me, and I held her eye for a moment.

"Look on the bright side. We thought we'd lost the packages. Now we're being taken straight to them."

Locke, from the far end of the bench, frowned at me, then laughed.

"I don't know whether to admire your resilience, Mason, or despair at your stupidity. But you'd be well advised to start resigning yourself to the fact it's all over for you. From now until the day you die, your life will be snow, ice, and hard labor. It's over, Mason."

A surge of hot anger welled up in my gut. I held his eye and asked him quietly, "What are your plans for next week, George?"

He arched an eyebrow. He was going to tell me to go to hell but decided to have some fun instead.

"Actually, I'm flying to Cuba for some well-earned rest

and relaxation. I'll send you a postcard if you let me know what camp you're in."

I shook my head. "No," I said. "You'll be dead before you get there."

For a moment, there was concern in his eyes, even fear. Then he sighed, muttered, "Get real," and looked away.

We headed north and east across Germany and Poland for three hours until we passed the port of Gdansk on the Baltic Sea and crossed the border into Kaliningrad, the westernmost outpost of the Russian empire.

SEVENTEEN

WE CROSSED THE BORDER TO THE SOUTH OF THE city of Kaliningrad, over the Vistula Lagoon, then turned east and followed the border to the large forest of Les Skvosznoy. We crossed the dense forest and, on the eastern side, spotted a couple of lakes and between them what appeared to be a 14th or 15th century castle, with tall white towers tipped by blue cones. There was no moat and no drawbridge, so we came down gradually on the ample lawns outside the main gate, making the fringe of trees on the woodland bow and toss.

As they unloaded us from the chopper, a couple of Jeeps emerged from the fortress, which from the ground looked more like a 19th century folly than an actual castle. They bundled us each in a separate Jeep and drove at speed back toward the castle.

Through the huge, arched gate with a portcullis suspended above us, we entered a cobbled courtyard, maybe a hundred and fifty foot square, with long staircases that climbed to the ramparts, doorways into the towers, and one vast arched door at the far end.

We sped across the courtyard to that double door, where the Jeeps skidded to a halt. We were bundled out of the Jeeps again and shoved and marched through the vast double doors.

We entered a large hall with a black stone floor and a domed ceiling which must have been three stories high. On the right, there was a marble fireplace at least six feet high and another six across. Passages branched off to right and left, and across the hall, tall stained glass windows showed images of tortured saints. On either side, dark mahogany staircases rose to a galleried landing that overlooked the hall. Here Locke turned to us and said, "I'll see you chaps later. I imagine by then you'll be in a lot of pain." He smiled. "I certainly hope so."

They marched us up the stairs and down a corridor on our left, where another stained glass window cast red and green light on the floor. The image was of a man tied to a post, skewered by arrows. One of the guards rapped on the door. It buzzed and opened, and we were shoved inside. The room was large, but the immensely high, domed ceiling gave the impression that it was vaster than it was. The walls were gray stone, though they were lined by books to a height of some six feet. An iron candelabra shaped like a wheel hung on a heavy chain from the center of the dome, and at the far end, dwarfed by the size of the room and everything else in it, was a desk, and sitting behind it was a wizened, twisted woman in a green uniform. Behind her, large logs blazed in a fireplace at least the size of the one downstairs.

We were shoved across the room to two bentwood chairs

in front of the desk and made to sit. While the guards cuffed us to the chairs, Colonel Alexandrina Vitsin lit a cigarette and inhaled the smoke deep through her open mouth. When they were done, she jerked her chin at the guards, and they left.

"Every time we meet in a castle, eh?" She leaned back and sucked again on her cigarette. In the half-light of the huge room, her eyes looked like small black holes onto nothing. "Last time Nero prisoner, then I prisoner, now you prisoner. We are all prisoner of space and pain, huh?"

I smiled. "I discuss these matters better with my hands un-cuffed and holding a glass of whiskey."

She ignored me, and her eyes grazed Gallin. "Beautiful woman. Beautiful Jewish woman. You saw fireplace downstairs, in hall? One time—" She sucked again on the cigarette, opened her mouth, and breathed all the way down. When she spoke again, the smoke came out in wafts with every word. "I want a woman to serve me as slave. She says me no, so I put her husband head in the fire. He is going crazy, kicking, screaming. She is screaming. Everybody screaming, but I am laughing. She will serve me as slave. He after cannot live. No use to nobody. So they shoot him."

"What a rich and inspiring life you lead, Colonel. And so young and attractive."

She closed her eyes and turned to me. "You want your head in fire, Mr. Mason? Then Captain Gallin can serve me as a slave."

"Colonel, this is all very amusing and entertaining. It reminds me of several movies I avoided seeing. One of them was *James Bond and the Cracked Dike*. It was about how an MI6 agent saved Holland. But in spite of your fascinating fantasies, with a PH, the Pentagon is going to want us home and unharmed sooner rather than later. In case you are wondering, I called Nero just before George picked us up in his helicopter."

She grinned. If an iguana could grin, it would grin like that. Her teeth were shades of amber and black, and her mouth was too long.

"You want your phone to call him again? Call him. Tell him *Come here, Papa, get me and Captain Gallin.*" Her laugh turned into a gurgling nicotine cough. "Maybe," she said as she stuck the butt in her mouth again. "Maybe he come get you."

Gallin spoke for the first time. "What do you want, Colonel?"

Vitsin arched her left eyebrow surprisingly high. "What does a woman like me want, huh? You are like me. You are similar like me. You want, I want. We want same things. Love, money, power." She grinned her ugly grin again. "Some fun. You don't want this?"

Behind her, the logs crackled and spat sparks.

I sighed. "If this theatrics is part of the torture, I have to tell you it's working. What do you want, Colonel? If you wanted us dead, you would have killed us in Belgium. You didn't. You went to the trouble of bringing us here. So what is it? What do you want?"

She lifted her shoulders, smiled, and looked around the room, up into the shadows of the domed ceiling, like divine, inspired words could be read there.

"Revenge," she said simply. "Making pain in you, and Captain Gallin, and in Nero. I want your pain to give me pleasure."

She sat staring at me for a moment. The burning end of her cigarette had almost reached her fingers. She stubbed it out in an overflowing ashtray and lit another, then she stood. One hand behind her back, the other holding her cigarette, she paced slowly to the end of her desk.

"You kill," she said. "All the time you kill, kill, kill." She stopped and smiled her ugly smile at me. "It's okay. I like to kill too. You cross the ultimate line of the forbidden. To watch a person end in your hands. Is good."

She turned and started pacing toward me. There was a hot coal in my belly, and it was hard to keep my eyes from the hot coal on the end of her cigarette.

She came and stood behind me. I could feel her presence inches from my back.

"But is power," she said. "Power is the big aphrodisiac, eh, Captain? When we kill, is not death that excites us, eh? It is magnificent power over another person. We make them nothing, and we are everything. Power is everything."

She went quiet, but I could hear her breathing, shallow and rapid. I felt her fingers on my shirt collar, touching the back of my neck.

"Big, strong man, but I have such power over him now, eh, Captain Gallin?"

Then the pain pierced my back, my shoulders, and my neck like a burning needle. I had known it was coming, and I had prepared myself. I didn't scream. I clenched my teeth and set my jaw, and as the smell of burning flesh reached my nostrils, I kept telling myself it had to stop. It had to stop soon. But each second was an eternity, and soon I heard her whimpering, with her hot breath in my ear.

And she stopped.

"Battle scars, Mr. Mason, very attractive to women."

I was trembling. I felt nauseated, and my head was swimming, and the pain in my neck and shoulder throbbed through me, making me dizzy. In the midst of all the pain and the nausea, some stupid part of my mind that thought it was clever said, "That all you got? No wonder the Soviet Union collapsed."

I felt her turn and braced myself for another dose. But then Gallin was shouting and I could hear real rage in her voice.

"*Shut up, Mason! Can't you for once just shut your goddamn mouth? Every fucking time you open your mouth, you think you're being so damned clever, but all you ever do is create more problems. Just shut up! For Christ's sake, shut up!*"

There was a ringing silence. I figured I'd take her advice and shut up for a while. Vitsin's stillness was like a physical presence in the room. She moved slowly away from me, came into view on my left, and moved back toward the desk. She sat.

Gallin spoke again, more quietly. "Don't go interpreting anything. We've been collaborating a while, and we are solid. So don't go getting ideas. We are stressed, and under stress you do and say things, right? I just wish he'd learn to shut his damned mouth."

Her voice was like a snake. "You care for him. You have feelings for him."

Gallin's laugh was harsh. "Have you ever *seen* an Israeli guy? Or woman for that matter—"

"I'm looking at one now."

"Yeah, funny. These are men and women who live on the

line every day. This Yankee doodle? No, it takes more than that, Colonel Vitsin, to make me have feelings."

"You are talking and talking and talking, Captain. You hope that while you are talking, I will not hurt your man. You think I am stupid."

"He's not my man, Colonel. He's a jerk, and I have applied to get transferred six times. But he's a colleague and an ally. I don't want him tortured. So I am asking you again. What do you want? If I can, I will give it to you. Just no more cigarette burns, please!"

"What do I want, what do I want. What do you want, Captain?"

"What do I want? I want to get the evidence you stole from us, I want to avoid Israel getting dragged into your damned third world war, and I want to go home to my beautiful boyfriend in London."

Vitsin snorted. "Forget the evidence. You can never have this. Israel—" She shrugged and spread her hands. "Politics, power, the Middle East, oil, and banks. Israel and the Arabs are at the heart of ninety percent of world conflict. Forget this. There is nothing you can do. But go home to your beautiful boyfriend. This, maybe we can do."

The silence that followed was a huge thing, a presence in the room pregnant with meaning and with menace. Eventually Gallin spoke, and her voice was barely a hiss.

"How...? What would you want in exchange?"

She jerked her head at me. "Kill him."

Another silence followed. Then Vitsin's voice filled the room like the crack of a whip. "You will not kill him. Not today, anyway. Maybe you will kill him when he fills you with pity and you want to stop his suffering. That I will enjoy. Or maybe you will kill him if it is a choice between him and Israel. This we cannot do today."

Gallin's voice was like steel when she answered. "You want me to kill him now? If I kill him now, will you send me back to London? What guarantee have I that you'll honor your word?"

Another silence. I leaned back in my chair. I felt bad, but I exaggerated it and snarled at Gallin, "You bitch. You'd do that too, wouldn't you?"

She screamed at me, and her face flushed red. Her neck swelled with corded tendons. "*Shut up, Mason! Shut up! Shut up! For Christ's sake shut up!*"

Colonel Vitsin spoke quietly. "I can give you no guarantees. Just as I can give you no weapon. Can you kill this man with your hands?"

"You know I was in the IDF. You know I can kill him with my hands."

"And then? How do you suggest, Captain Gallin, that I guarantee your safe return to London or Tel Aviv?"

Gallin's voice had dropped barely to a whisper. "If I work for you..."

The colonel rang a bell on her desk. The door opened, and four guards came in. She waved a dismissive hand at us, and the guards released us from the chairs and dragged us out of the room.

They took us down a passage to a bare room with a stone floor and stone walls. There was no window. There was one electric bulb in the ceiling, out of reach. The door slammed shut. I sank to the floor, but Gallin remained standing by the door.

"We should have planned it. I told you we needed an

extraction plan." Her eyes were venomous. "But you and your stupid, reckless American *go in with guns blazing and it will all work out*! You always believe Uncle Sam will come galloping in with the seventh bloody cavalry. Well where's your damned cavalry now, Mason?"

"Leave me alone, will you? I never thought I'd see the day. You are willing to *kill me?*" I allowed my voice to become shrill. "You are willing to *kill me?* Did you hear yourself in there? We are supposed to be friends, Gallin! Not just allies and colleagues, but friends! Have you forgotten the times I have saved your life? And you are willing to kill me? Just so you can get back to your damned boyfriend?"

"Have you any idea how *sick* I am of you, Mason? Have you any idea the number of times I have applied to have this secondment revoked? Do you have *any* idea how *sick* I am of your unprofessional, cavalier attitude? Saved my life? What about all the times you have put it at risk? And now you have finally achieved it. We are going to die in here. First they'll torture you to death to try and break me, and then I'll have to chose between working for them as a double agent or being raped and murdered. And all because of your stupid, American lack of professionalism. Thanks, Mason. Thanks a lot." She slid down the wall to the floor and started whispering to herself. "God, I hate you, Mason. What you have done to us. God, I hate you so much, you stupid son of a bitch. God, I hate you..." A short while after that, she started to weep quietly.

EIGHTEEN

I don't know how many hours they kept us there. It felt like days. They didn't feed us, and they gave us nothing to drink, and by the time the doors opened again, we were in pretty bad shape. They dragged us to our feet. Gallin was trembling and looked like she could be turning feverish. I was feeling bad, but I made out I was worse than I was. Not because I had any kind of plan, but just because it's always a good idea to have your enemy think you're weaker than you are.

They took us down the corridor again, back to Colonel Vitsin's office. No light shone through the stained glass windows we passed on the way, and when we entered her office, the glass in the tall, gabled windows was black. She was sitting in the same place, with the fire crackling behind her. In my weakened, dehydrated state, the tips of the flames that licked up behind her head seemed diabolical.

Gallin spoke first as we stood in front of her desk.

"I need water."

Vitsin jerked her chin at the guards. They forced us into our chairs, and one of them placed a carafe of water on the table in front of us. I was about to go for it, but two of the guards rammed me back and cuffed me to the chair. Gallin went to move, but the guard on her right pulled his Glock and placed it to Gallin's head.

Vitsin spoke. "Peace, for you, Captain, is so close. Peace and satisfaction. All it requires from you is a small step in your mind. I own you. I own both of you. You are my property. This is simple reality. What changes for you is this. If you fight the truth, you suffer. If you accept the truth, much pleasure can come your way. Realize and accept that you belong to me, and peace will come." She laughed. "And water."

She was pale and drawn, and I could see her hands trembling. She said, "What do I have to do?"

"I need your obedience. First you will tell me exactly what, in your mind, what is our relationship. The relationship between you, Captain, and me. What is our relationship?"

Gallin sat for a long moment staring at the carafe of water. She kept swallowing and making an ugly, pasty noise with her mouth. Finally she said, "You own me. I am your property. And however much I hate it, you can do with me, and my life, whatever you please. Because you own the power of violence. And I must serve you."

Vitsin threw back her head and laughed out loud. "Good, good! Fantastic! Give her a glass of water. Sip it, Captain, or you will become ill. Sip, sip."

A guard had stepped forward and poured her a glass of water. I watched it, and my whole body was nothing more than the craving for that water. Somewhere inside my mind, I fought to stay in control. I forced myself to think that if we were this badly dehydrated, we must have been at least twenty-four hours without fluids. We had arrived in late afternoon, but outside it was dark. So it could have been thirty-six hours or more.

Gallin was sipping, trying to keep control of her hand and the powerful drive to drain the glass. It was hard, watching her, to stay focused on what Vitsin was saying.

"And now you expect me to believe what you say? Oh, you are my servant, you obey me, you do everything and anything I say! All for a little water and a soft bed."

Gallin drained the last traces of fluid and glared at the colonel.

"What do you expect, Colonel? Love? There is no love in this world, and you know it! The most you will ever get from me is loyalty through self-interest and honesty! If you expect me to get on my knees and tell you I love you and you are some kind of goddess, well, yeah. I'll do it! But you will know that I am just obeying orders." She pointed a finger at her. "But know this. If I have to work for you to protect my country and my people, I will do it, and I will do it professionally and with loyalty. I am *good* at what I do and I have *my* self-respect! You have me. You own me. Okay, that's the reality. But let's stay out of fantasy land."

"Very good, Captain. Very good…" She fished a cigarette out of her pack and took her time lighting it. She inhaled noisily through gritted teeth, then blew out the smoke at the ceiling. "You will, in time, come to love me and adore me. They all do. But for now, your honesty and loyalty are enough."

Gallin leaned forward. "I don't know how many hours you had us lying on that stone floor..."

"Thirty-five hours. You are both strong, in your mind and your body. Normal people are hysterical after three or four hours. Dehydration makes it much worse. No position is good. Everything hurts. The pressure of the stone is unendurable, and the dehydration makes everything a hundred times more sensitive. You are strong, both strong."

She was looking at me with hooded eyes. I said, "I will kill Captain Gallin with my bare hands if you will just give me a glass of water. I will tell you everything and anything you want to know. I just, please, I need some water."

She turned her gaze on Gallin. "He is pathetic. He was strong, very strong, but now? He is spineless, weak, a nothing."

Gallin said with great deliberation, "What do I need to do to get a bed, water, and food?"

Vitsin watched her, reading her face, her tone, her gestures. She kept her eyes on Gallin but jerked her chin at me.

"Kill him."

"Is that all? I do that and you will give me a bed and water, and food."

"Yes."

"And then I start my induction? When can I go back to London?"

"Kill him, then we will talk."

"I use my hands?"

"Yes. Just your hands." She grinned. "Maybe feet, elbows, knees, teeth..."

Gallin turned to me. There were tears in her eyes, but

her look was cold. Her eyes were ruthless, and her jaw was set.

"I'm sorry, Mason. You brought this on yourself with your stupidity and your hubris. You messed up, and this is how it ends."

I snarled at her, "Cuffed to a chair and dehydrated. That's the only way you stand a chance. Just get close enough and I'll kill you, even chained to this chair..."

I trailed off, like waves of delirium were washing over me. Gallin stood. She moved toward me, and then behind me.

"You want a quick execution? Or you want a show of loyalty?"

I saw the corner of Vitsin's mouth twitch.

"If you are offering a show, I cannot say no."

Gallin's voice came again. "Hold him! Keep him straight!"

Vitsin snapped a translation in Russian, and I felt strong arms grip me and force me back and upright in the chair. I closed my eyes and gritted my teeth.

I didn't see it because she was standing behind me. The two guards had grabbed my upper arms and hauled me back to the chair. I had closed my eyes and braced myself for whatever was coming next. What came next were two screams. One was a savage, brutal scream from Gallin as she lashed out with a cruel sidekick. The next was a scream of deep agony as her heel connected with the knee of the guard on my right, and his cartilage broke and he fell to the floor beside me.

She didn't pause. She wasn't that kind of girl. As her foot hit the ground, she stepped in to the guard on my left and rammed the middle knuckles of her folded fingers into his trachea, breaking the cartilage and putting him into a chocking spasm.

By now, I had opened my eyes and was staring hard at Vitsin, whose mouth hung open. Barely a second had passed since she'd told the guards to hold me still. Now I heard the slip of steel on leather as she pulled the choking guard's 443 Grach from his holster. She didn't shoot him with it. She smashed the but into the back of his neck, snapping his spinal cord. Then, pointing it at Vitsin, she stepped around and stamped on the back of the other guard's neck.

"Press the alarm, call your guards," she said to Vitsin, whose right hand was reaching for her top drawer, "do anything stupid, and whatever happens to me and Mason afterwards, you will be dead. Because I will shoot you in the head and heart without hesitation. So let's just keep it quiet and friendly."

Keeping the Grach aimed at the colonel, she felt in the guards' pockets and found the keys to my cuffs. She released me, and while I grabbed the carafe and slurped water into my mouth, she went around the desk, grabbed a handful of Vitsin's hair, and pulled her around to where I had been sitting. The colonel was doing a bizarre dance with her skinny legs and arms, clenching her teeth and trying not to scream. Gallin had the weapon rammed in the back of her neck and was snarling, "Scream. Go on, scream!"

She shoved her in the chair and gave her a back hander that must have sent the room spinning. To me, she said, "You done drinking? Cuff her to the chair while I cover her."

I put the carafe down, grabbed the other dead guard's weapon, shoved it in my waistband, behind my back, and set about cuffing the colonel to the chair where I had been just seconds before. I was about to ask her where the evidence packages were, but then I thought about what she had put Gallin through, Gallin had earned the right to ask the questions.

She put her own weapon in her waistband, took hold of the carafe, and threw what little water was left in the colonel's face. The colonel spluttered and groaned. Gallin hunkered down in front of her with a hand on each arm of the chair.

"I'm going to tell you what I am going to do, Colonel. I am going to suffocate you. I don't know how yet. I'll look for a plastic bag or some tape or something. I bet you have all that kind of stuff in here, right? But if I don't find anything, I will just stuff your mouth full of your guards' socks and pinch your nose until you turn blue."

She stood and looked down at her a moment, while I set about removing the guards' boots and socks. Gallin went on.

"I don't want to kill you. Not yet. Because you are our ticket out of here. Without you, we are going to have a real problem getting into Poland. So you are more useful to me alive. But..." She glanced at me as I made a big ball of the socks. "More important than that is getting that evidence you received in Brussels. You tell me where that is, and you live to get us out of here. You don't and you suffocate to death."

She gave me the nod, and with my left hand I prized her mouth open while with my right I stuffed the four balled socks in. It's not something I am proud of, and it's a moment in my life I would like to forget. Her screams were smothered by the balled cloth, and by the time Gallin pinched her nose, her lungs were empty from trying to scream. Within seconds, she was convulsing, thrashing and twisting in the chair. I began to worry she's have a cardiac arrest, but Gallin was bent over, staring into her face with her thumb and finger clenched on her nose. After a few more seconds, she started to turn purple, and Gallin released her and pulled the socks from her mouth. As she croaked and drew in air noisily through her mouth, Gallin put the pistol to her head and said, "Scream for the guards and you'll die in a tenth of a second."

We gave her thirty seconds to recover her breath, and Gallin gave me the nod again and pinched her nose. Before I had my fingers on her jaw, she was saying, "*No! No! I tell! I tell!*"

"Where?"

"In safe. Behind Putin picture on wall by fire."

A savage expression twisted Gallin's face, and she snatched hold of the colonel's nose again and twisted. "Combination?"

Vitsin made a horrible, high-pitched, nasal squeaking noise that turned into "*Three two, three two, three two!*"

Gallin went to the picture of Putin and took it down from where it hung on the wall. Behind it, there was a safe built into the wall. I placed the muzzle of the Grach against the colonel's knee and pressed. Gallin spun the dials, and I guess the old truism is true that those who dish it out can very rarely take it. Because the door of the safe swung open. Inside there was a black attaché case. Gallin closed the safe and placed the Putin picture back, then carried the case to the desk. She flipped the latches, and it opened. Two minutes showed that it was what we had been after.

I gave Gallin a rueful smile. "Did somebody say extraction plan?"

The corners of her mouth twitched. "Watch and learn how it's done, big guy."

She went over to Vitsin and hunkered down in front of her. In a sudden, savage movement, she squeezed her mouth open and stuffed the socks in again. Vitsin began to panic. Gallin drew her face real close.

"You smoke too much. That's why your lungs can't get enough oxygen. Try to relax and breathe slowly."

She waited a moment while Vitsin struggled to control her breathing. Then she nodded.

"That's right. Now I'll tell you what I am going to do. I am going to break your nose with the butt of this gun. And you will choke and suffocate on your own blood."

Vitsin was shaking her head, and her face was creasing into sobbing. She had had enough. Gallin nodded.

"If I don't kill you, Colonel, your own people will for letting this evidence get away. Let's face it; you are finished."

She shook her head and wept some more. I was almost moved to compassion and had to keep reminding myself what this woman did for fun and relaxation.

Gallin said, "There is one thing you can do to save your skin. You come with us and act as a witness to corroborate this evidence. Do that and you live. I'll tell you something else. Knowing the kind of people they have in Central Intelligence, you'll probably even get a four-bedroom condo by the sea in Malibu, overlooking the beach. And isn't that just what you deserve, after everything you have done for humanity? A whole new start in life."

NINETEEN

At the top of the thirteen stone steps that run down from the main entrance of the International Court of Justice in the Hague, before the nine great arches that form the façade of that building, there had gathered a rabble of reporters. Facing them was a small group of worried men and women: court administrators, the current president of the court, Mohammed Rahman, and the European Commissioner for Crisis Management, Leo Wolfe.

It was Wolfe who was addressing the reporters in this impromptu and unorthodox press conference.

"Please, please, the situation right now is that we have received evidence that alleges certain actions on the part of the British Government, assisted by Israel. If, and I do stress *if* these allegations were to be proved to be true, it would mean that those responsible would be in serious breach of well-established international laws enshrined in international conventions. However, this evidence, which has been brought to me and entrusted to me, to be delivered to the International Court of Justice, has yet to be analyzed and studied with great care, not just by the legal experts who compose our current panel of fifteen judges of the highest standing, but also by forensic experts to ensure that there has been no tampering, and that the evidence is authentic."

One of the reporters called, "Is there any reason, Commissioner, to believe the evidence may be false?"

The commissioner ignored the question and stepped aside. Mohammed Rahman, the president of the court, approached the microphones.

"In a case such as this, with such profound, potential repercussions, it is of the greatest importance to establish beyond any possible doubt the authenticity of the evidence.

"We heard last week that the Russian government made allegations against the British secret services that they had engineered an allegedly Islamic attack on Moscow. At that time, no evidence was adduced that this was the case, and the British government denied the accusation.

"Now Commissioner Leo Wolfe has approached us, and he has informed us that evidence has been passed to him, as an objective third party, which claims to prove the Russian allegations, but also goes much further and implicates Israel and the Israeli Mossad and IDF in this alleged attack.

"As Commissioner Wolfe has pointed out, at this stage, these are simply allegations, which Britain and Israel reject very forcefully. It is now for the court to analyze the evidence in depth and make a study and an assessment of its content."

He paused a moment, the continued with extreme gravity.

"The implications of these allegations are profound and

far-reaching. I would therefore ask the press to exercise the greatest restraint and maturity in your reporting. Nothing— I repeat *nothing*—has been proved. All we have are allegations made in an extremely volatile environment. Please let us avoid any unnecessary escalation."

That had been at nine o'clock in the morning. By noon, the news had spread across the world, and in London, New York, Paris, and Berlin, spontaneous demonstrations had erupted in the streets, with chants demanding justice for Palestinians and punishment for Britain and Israel. Putin and the Iranian ayatollahs joined the fray, demanding loudly and forcefully that the severest sanctions be imposed on the guilty parties, and in the United States, an unverified statement was attributed to Donald Trump to the effect that, "The last thing America needs now is to go to war with Russia to bail out the Brits. We don't need Britain and we don't need NATO."

To which Macron allegedly replied, "Europe does not need the UK or the USA!"

Though they both later denied making these statements and attributed them to fake news and even AI, the die was cast, and the idea was now out in the open. The USA could survive without NATO. NATO could survive without the USA, and nobody needed the UK.

While this virus spread across the world, sowing the seeds of impending violence, Commissioner Leo Wolfe and Mohammed Rahman, the president of the ICJ, withdrew into the Palace of Peace to the president's chambers. There they sat and drank coffee. Their conversation was desultory, and even the normally gregarious commissioner was subdued, with his attention focused internally upon his own thoughts.

At half past ten a.m., there was a tap at the door, and the judge's secretary opened it and stepped in.

"Colonel Georgie Loktev, sir."

The judge sat erect. "Ah, send him in!"

The commissioner set down his cup and took a deep breath. Colonel Georgie Loktev, the man known to the British Secret Intelligence Service as George Locke, entered the room as the others rose to greet him. They shook hands warmly, but the commissioner gave a laugh that was on the tense side of cordial and gestured at the colonel's hands.

"My dear colonel, what a pleasure to see you at last, but I note that you come with empty hands!"

The colonel sat and smiled. "My dear chap," he said in his flawless English. "Please don't worry. Colonel Alexandrina Vitsin is on her way, and"—his smile broadened—"she is bringing substantially more than we had hoped for."

The commissioner and the judge glanced at each other.

"She brings not only documents provided by the FSB demonstrating British and Israeli collaboration, but she brings two prisoners as well."

Mohammed Rahman frowned. "Prisoners?"

"Arrested in Kaliningrad during an assassination attempt. They are an American and an Israeli. He is from some black ops organization connected with the Pentagon, and she is from the Mossad. They will provide testimony as to the authenticity of the evidence we have accumulated."

The commissioner said, "Mason and Captain Gallin?"

"The very same."

"Excellent work, Colonel."

"We caught them attempting to assassinate the colonel. We interrogated them in Kaliningrad, and they are on their way now." He smiled with hooded eyes, looking at the floor. "Colonel Vitsin gave them the opportunity to reflect on their mistakes. They saw the error of their ways, and so the colonel has said to me in a phone call just an hour ago, they are prepared to make statements to the court." He glanced at his watch. "They should be arriving in the next fifteen to twenty minutes."

The room fell silent, with the three men staring at each other. Mohammed Rahman said, "This is unexpected progress."

Commissioner Leo Wolfe looked at Rahman, then at Locke, and erupted in an outburst of laughter. The other two watched him and were soon contaminated by his mirth and began to laugh too.

TWENTY

We touched down at Vliegbasis Gilze Rijen airfield at eleven a.m. and were hauled to our feet by the four paramilitary cops who had traveled with us. Colonel Alexandrina Vitsin, clutching her attaché case, watched without expression as we were shoved off the helicopter and into the unmarked Range Rovers with smoked windows that sat waiting for us. I was shoved into the lead vehicle with Gallin and Vitsin, two armed guards, and the driver. Four more guards got into the rear truck, and we took off at speed.

It was a little over fifty miles, and we made it in a little over forty-five minutes. We sped through the gates of the court and stopped outside the main entrance, contrary to protocol but in accordance with the Benelux governments' desire to make a public show of what was going down. Members of the press and the media, unofficially alerted to our arrival, filmed and took photographs as we were pushed up the stairs. Some called out questions, but we ignored them and kept our heads down.

The seven guards gathered around us, one of them clutching a large case he had extracted from the trunk of the rear Range Rover. They marched us up the stairs, pushing away reporters who got too close, but not so aggressively that they would give up. The footage and the commentary was going out worldwide, and that was something everybody wanted.

We were marched through the door and then led at a quick march to the chambers of the president of the court, Mohammed Rahman. Colonel Vitsin stepped to the door and knocked. The president's secretary opened the door and smiled.

"Colonel Vitsin, they are expecting you. Please follow me."

Two of the guards took up their posts beside the door. The other five followed us across the broad anteroom. The secretary opened a second, heavy oak door and announced, "Colonel Vitsin, sir, with the prisoners."

Two more of the paramilitaries took up posts beside the judge's door, and Vitsin led Gallin and me and the three remaining guards into the large office.

Commissioner Leo Wolfe was reclining in an armchair, laughing. George Locke was standing by the window, smiling, with his hands thrust into his pockets. The judge had adopted a grave, appropriately judicial expression from behind his vast desk. He stood and extended a hand across the desk to Colonel Vitsin.

"Colonel, this is indeed an unexpected and happy surprise. I have to say we were all expecting a more protracted struggle. But if what George tells me is correct, then our case is well on its way."

Vitsin directed her gaze at George. He said, "Colonel, such a pleasure to see you again."

She turned her gaze on Wolfe, who merely said, "Madam."

"Please, take a seat." It was Rahman speaking again. "Can I offer you a drink, coffee, tea..."

"I do not require a drink, judge. I bring prisoners to make initial statement before witnesses. We have bring recording equipment. I will hand over to you the conclusive evidence against MI6, Mossad, and British and Israeli governments when recording equipment is running."

The guard with the case had opened it and was setting up a tripod and a video camera, along with sound recording equipment.

"I provide you also, judge, evidence of attempted murder of me twice. One time when they think I am in car going from Brussels to the Hague, and second time when they invade my office in Kaliningrad. She"—she pointed to Gallin—"is telling that she is Mossad, but she is seconded to MI6. He is CIA and seconded to ultra secret department of Pentagon. Finally, war crimes and crimes against humanity of United States and United Kingdom can be exposed for world to see. When I will give you the evidence, then you will question them. I give you copy of film, other copy goes to Vladimir." She paused an expressionless second and added, "Vladimir Putin."

She delivered the whole thing without the smallest trace of passion or emotion. By the time she was done, the paramilitary with the camera had finished too. She looked at him. He nodded and started the camera.

We all watched her as she stood, with a strange, jerky

thrust of her legs, and crossed the five feet to the desk. There she thrust out her hand, clutching the attaché case. Rahman had stood to receive it and took it from her hands and laid it in front of him. His lips trembled and broke into a smile as he flipped the catches and opened the lid.

"So!" he said and sat, gesturing at the folders of documents, the photographs and the pen drives loaded with videos. "So," he said again, nodding. "Mr. Mason, Captain Aila Gallin, what? What have you to say?"

I said, "Is that a rhetorical question? Because right now, we are surrounded by hostile witnesses, and you are interrogating witnesses."

It was Commissioner Leo Wolfe who answered.

"Come, Mr. Mason, let us be mature and grown up. I invited you to dinner, laid on quite a feast, though I say so myself, and gave you ample and generous warning of the results if you persisted in your pursuit." He laughed out loud and looked over at Locke. "The Rule of Law means something quite different here in the European Union, you know. Here it means that the law rules. You have been arrested, and you are here before one of the most senior judges on the planet. You cannot question his authority. If he judges it is reasonable to question you, then who the hell are you to question his authority?"

I ignored him and turned to Rahman. "The International Court of Justice does not belong to the European Union. You represent the United Nations. You have accountability. You cannot interrogate suspects in private session when those suspects are surrounded by hostile witnesses."

"You are an intelligent, educated man, Mr. Mason." He

spread his hands and blinked his large, dark eyes. "You know that in law, the truth does not exist. Only facts exist in the law. And what is a fact? A fact is something that you can prove before a court of law. So tell me, Mr. Mason, Captain Gallin, tell me how can you prove—how will you ever prove —that this"—he gestured all around him—"that this ever happened?"

I gave him the sourest look I could muster. "It's on camera," I said.

That made him laugh some more. "I think you heard as well as I did, Mr. Mason, that this movie is meant as a memento for the good judge Rahman, for me and for Mr. Putin. The world is changing, Mr. Mason. The Age of the Common Man is coming to an end. The cross of accountability is finally cast off, and the powerful are once again masters of the world."

Gallin's face was screwed up into a ball. "Do you *ever* stop talking shit, Wolfe?" She turned to Rahman and then Locke. "Can you shut him up?"

The judge scowled at her. "You would be well advised to watch your tongue, Captain Gallin. You know what Arabs are liable to do to a Jewess with an overactive, insolent tongue."

"Why don't you tell me, Rahman? You have a background in Sharia."

His eyes were growing bright with anger. He leaned forward with his hands on his desk. "Yes, *Captain*, I have a background in Sharia, and a woman like you would have her tongue cut out. And it will be my pleasure to execute that judgment! Now let us cut to the chase. Make your confessions! Or would you prefer to return to Kaliningrad for some further reflection and contemplation?"

The all laughed again. I said, "Okay, I'll give you my confession, but I have one question I want to ask."

The judge snapped, "No questions! We ask the questions!"

I ignored him and looked at Locke. "You shot the four witnesses in Ukraine. You used a subsonic .22s with a suppressor. You went to all that trouble, so why didn't you use a revolver? Why did you leave shells with the Russian brand on them lying there to be found?"

He chuckled. "You really are stupid, aren't you, in the West? If I had used Western ammunition, or if I had not left spent shells, it would have pointed indisputably to somebody in the camp. Clearly the SAS were beyond suspicion, so that would have left me. The Russian casings created the doubt. Simple. Now, Mason, your confession for the camera."

"So you were the leak at MI6."

"Your confession, Mason!"

I turned to Rahman and then Leo Wolfe. "How far has the rot gone, Wolfe? There were times when you and your gang knew about our movements in advance, and Locke couldn't have known about it. How far does the rot go?"

It was Locke who answered again. "We had your cars bugged in the UK. You were easy to follow."

I kept my eyes on Wolfe. "It's not enough. You had penetrated deep, hadn't you?"

"My dear Mason, I am going to answer your question. Then I am going to smash one of Mr. Rahman's Waterford crystal glasses, and every time you refuse to give your confession, I am going to apply an exquisite cut to Captain Gallin's exquisite skin."

He stood and moved to a credenza against the wall, where he took a whiskey tumbler and smashed it against the side.

"It goes," he said, "very, very high up. You were negligent in your research, Mr. Mason. As soon as you began to suspect, as soon as I alerted you to the European Union's shifting allegiances, you should have done your research into who supported Brexit and who was in favor of remaining. You would be amazed at how deep that went with the Brits."

He stepped up close to Gallin and stroked her face with the broken tumbler.

"Now, Mason, we would not want to spoil this great beauty, would we, not until we have finished with her at least."

I looked at Rahman. "You, the president of the International Court of Justice, are going to allow this?"

He stood, came around the desk, made a noise like he was clearing his throat, and spat at my feet. "I am the president of the International Court of Justice, Mr. Mason, yes, but I am first a Muslim, and like every Muslim, jihad is sacred to me. We have you. Now we prove MI6 and Mossad's complicity, the UK and Israel's complicity in the murder of innocent people, subjugation of Palestine, attacks on Russia. It is all here." He pointed at the case. "And finally, the cherry on the icing on the cake: your confessions."

I nodded several times and finally said, "Yeah, okay, I'll confess. You all know—you, holding the sacred office of the president of the International Court of *Justice* and the Peace Palace—you all know that these confessions of mine and

Captain Gallin's were extracted by torture and are a pack of lies—"

Captain Vitsin had been staring at the floor while I spoke. Now she interrupted me. Her speech was wooden, rigid, almost like she was having a stroke while she was speaking.

"Shut up, Alex Mason, no more acting and procrastinating. You are prisoner, we, Commissioner Leo Wolfe, Colonel Georgie Loktev of Federal Security Service, and I, Colonel Alexandrina Vitsin, have you here, now, at chambers of Judge Mohammed Rahman, in Peace Palace International Court of Justice, with case full of evidence that MI6 and Mossad, UK and Israel conspire to commit atrocities. Yes, evidence is false, engineered by me with collaboration from Wolfe and Loktev and Rahman, but nothing you can do, so shut up and confessing or we torture you more."

There was a leaden silence as we all stared at her. Rahman was frowning hard. Wolfe had his eyes narrowed and lowered his broken glass, and Locke had frozen where he stood, leaning against the wall beside the window.

I said, "Okay, I'll confess. Vitsin told me I should say I mediated between the CIA, MI6, and the Mossad. Is that what you want me to say?"

I looked at Wolfe. For a moment, he said nothing, then, "Yes, say this." He looked at Gallin. "And you."

Gallin said, "Okay, I was told to say I received instructions from MI6 on how to help recruit a team to enter Moscow." She looked at Judge Rahman. "Is that what you want me to say?"

He stared at her a long moment. Then his eyes went wide. He stared at the guard beside me and pointed a trembling finger at the paramilitary at the camera. When he spoke, he screeched like a parrot, "*Kill him! Kill them!*"

The guard didn't move, but George Locke reached inside his pocket and pulled out a Glock 17.

I had my Sig out of my waistband before he took aim at Vitsin and put two slugs into his chest. Simultaneously I saw his head whiplash as Gallin's slugs hit home.

It should have ended there.

But suddenly there was a horrific shriek, and Colonel Vitsin sprang from her seat and lunged at the desk. She sprawled across it, knocking the attaché case flying, and grabbed the long, slim stiletto Rahman used as a paper opener. I saw his eyes go wide, and he shrieked too. Then Vitsin was on her feet. Her eyes were huge, but her pupils were pinpricks. Her mouth was huge and wide open in a scream as she rushed me, the dagger held low. I smelled the stench of tobacco on her stale breath, saw her tombstone amber and black teeth. I felt the blade closing on my belly. Over her shoulder, I was vaguely aware of Rahman moving, screaming like Vitsin. It all happened in fractions of seconds.

I pulled the trigger. The world exploded. Vitsin stopped dead, staring into my eyes. She frowned like that wasn't supposed to have happened. The paper knife dropped and clattered on the floor. Her throat rattled stench, and she fell.

I turned and saw two guards wrestling with Leo Wolfe, who lay on his back on the floor, kicking his feet, thrashing, and squealing. It was fractions of seconds. I turned to look for Gallin and the cameraman. The cameras was there, but Gallin and the cameraman were gone.

I took a step. The cameraman was on the floor too, curled in the fetus position with a pool of blood underneath him. His holster was empty. There was movement in the corner. The next fraction of a second was an eternity. I registered Gallin on her back. Rahman was straddling her. He had a semi-automatic raised like a hammer and was pounding down. Then his elbow went up and the muzzle aimed down, and I heard a horrible scream that filled the world.

I don't know how I moved. I levitated, and a monstrous burn in my belly seemed to propel me across the ten or twelve feet that separated us. I was not going for Rahman, because I knew a collision would trigger the shot. I was hurtling for the space between the gun and Gallin. And I hit it as he squeezed the trigger. The hammer struck. The world exploded again, and flame and molten lead burned into my side. I slumped onto Gallin's prone body. I felt her cheek against mine. Her left arm encircled me, and her right reached over my shoulder. Two cracks broke the silence that had engulfed me, and blackness closed in.

TWENTY-ONE

I was on a sofa, and my face was wet. When I opened my eyes, I saw Gallin smiling at me. She had a glass of water in her hand and was wiping my face with a wet cloth.

"Hey, welcome back."

"You're okay."

"Thanks."

"No, I mean..." I smiled. "You're not hurt."

"Neither are you. You have a nasty graze and a burn. But you'll live. We have company."

I sat up and looked around. There were medics, stretchers, men in uniform. Behind the desk was Nero, looking massive, watching me with a frown creasing his brow. A little to his left, at the end of the desk, was Sir Lacklan, watching me with no expression on his face at all. His blue eyes seemed to be calculating, but that was it.

He said, "You killed Locke."

The burning pain in my side made me wince. "Colonel Georgie Loktev. He was a double agent. Maybe a triple agent. The European Union was working with Russia to engineer this. Where's Wolfe?"

Gradually, the guys with the stretchers and the uniforms bustled and filed out of the room and closed the door so that Gallin and I were alone with Nero and Sir Lacklan.

Nero said, "On his way to the British Embassy in the company of Captain Eddy 'Spud' Walker. The Dutch and Belgian governments are falling over themselves to cooperate, as is the European Commission. The ICJ is of course at pains to assure us it had no idea of Mohammed Rahman's past connections with Sharia law and al-qaeda, or with Moscow."

"They were very bold," I said. He nodded. "As well they might be. The world is terrified of them, and the West's obsession with inclusiveness seems to have robbed the most intelligent, educated people of the capacity to think critically and discriminate."

"What about the attaché case of evidence and the film in the camera?"

"We recorded everything back at Headquarters, and we have secured the camera and the chip."

I nodded. "Good."

"You did well to contact me from Kaliningrad and arrange this. It was very satisfactory."

Sir Lacklan sighed. "A close call," he said. "We used to worry about having secrets stolen. Now it seems we have slipped into times when the future of mankind is forever in the balance." He held my eye a moment, then gazed at

Gallin. "We approach nine billion people on this planet at dizzying speed, global temperatures are steadily rising, regardless of whose fault it is, and AI becomes ever more clever and self-assertive. And in the midst of this madness, politicians grow ever more insane."

He turned and looked at Nero. "It is hard sometimes to know which way to turn, old chap. Are we better staying small and going our own way, like Iceland, or should we seek support from the great superstates, like America?"

I said, without looking at him, "Or Russia, or Europe."

"I have always believed there was strength in unity."

Nero said, "There are many kinds of strength, Lacklan. The kind of strength you get from unity requires the sacrifice of independence. Independence and self-sufficiency give you a different kind of strength."

Sir Lacklan nodded. "I suppose you're right, Nero. Belonging means you lose yourself, doesn't it? And ultimately you must sacrifice all you are and all you believe in to that faceless master, the Union."

Nero nodded once. "Orwell taught us that a long time ago."

I said, "Did you vote for Brexit, Sir Lacklan?"

He didn't meet my eye. "I'm afraid I didn't," he said. "I voted against it. I voted to remain."

"You believed in the Union."

"I believed in the European dream. A united world at peace. No poverty, no hunger, no more war."

Gallin said, "No freedom."

He looked at her. "Freedom. A word."

She said, "An aspiration. Perhaps an unachievable one but still worth fighting for."

He sighed heavily. "I always believed we would inevitably return home to Europe. I thought a serious threat from Russia would make that happen."

Nero said, "Europe was going its own way. Is still going its own way. Its path leads to the suppression of the individual and into the collective idea of the Union." He levered himself out of the chair and stood, gigantic behind the desk, looking down at Sir Lacklan. "You forgot, Lacklan, that the state is there to serve the individual. The individual is not the servant, much less the slave of the state. You lost your way, and I am sorry for that."

He came around the desk and stood in front of Gallin. He seemed to speak directly to her, though his words were intended for Sir Lacklan.

"The fragile balance of power has been temporarily restored. Though it is true that times of even greater chaos are coming. We will be sorely challenged in the coming years. The fragile jewel of democracy and the rule of law will be in serious peril. It is possible we will not be able to preserve them. Our future, the future of our children, may be ugly and dystopian. It is important for us to keep a clear mind, a clear intention, and to fight always for what is good. Otherwise we stand to lose everything and descend into a new Dark Ages of physical, mental, and spiritual tyranny. Do you understand that?"

Gallin was frowning. She nodded. "Yes."

He turned to me. "Do you understand that?"

I screwed up my face and said, "Yes."

He turned back to Sir Lacklan, and he had a Sig Sauer in his hand. He raised it. Sir Lacklan watched him impassively a moment, then closed his eyes, as though in prayer. Nero pulled the trigger and placed a single shot in the middle of his brow. Sir Lacklan sagged back into his chair. A thread of red blood crawled down to his right eye.

Nero turned to us. "I shall see you both back in Virginia for debriefing."

He moved massively to the door, opened it, and left. Gallin stared at the door. I was staring at Sir Lacklan's dead body, thinking that he had died not because he was a bad man but because he was misguided.

Gallin took a deep breath and stood. She reached down for me and helped me to my feet.

"Come on, big guy. Let's get the hell out of here."

Outside, down on the steps, where cops were milling and carefully ignoring us, we stood outside the nine great arches of the Palace of Peace. I paused a moment and looked down at Gallin. She smiled up at me, and I thought how beautiful she was, but how that beauty was not just about her perfect, dark features, but how it radiated from inside: intelligent, animal, and alive. I gave her a squeeze and said, "When we get back, you know what? I am going to let you drive my car."

She gave me a painful smack on the chest and grinned. "Really? Are you serious? That so funny," she said, and we started to climb down the thirteen steps of the temple. "Because I had decided I was going to let you sleep with me!"

"This again." I shook my head as I limped down to the square. "How many times do I have to tell you? I don't want to sleep with you. Is there anything less interesting that you can do with a person than sleep with them?"

"Well, okay, we can sit in the same bed and play cards or

Scrabble. Or I can read you the newspapers, or *The Lord of the Rings*..."

"Now you're talking..." I said, and she linked her arm through mine.

DON'T MISS ANYTHING!

If you want to stay up to date on all new releases in this series, with these authors, or with any of our new deals, you can do so by joining our newsletters below.

In addition, you will immediately gain access to our entire *Right House VIP Library*, which currently includes *ORIGINS*—a full length prequel novel to *ODIN*.

righthouse.com/email

(Easy to unsubscribe. No spam. Ever.)

ALSO BY DAVID ARCHER

Up to date books can be found at:
www.righthouse.com/david-archer

ROGUE THRILLERS
Gates of Hell (Book 1)
Hell's Fury (Book 2)

JACOB HUNTER THRILLERS
The Kyiv File (Book 1)
The Bogota File (Book 2)

PETER BLACK THRILLERS
Burden of the Assassin (Book 1)
The Man Without A Face (Book 2)
Unpunished Deeds (Book 3)
Hunter Killer (Book 4)
Silent Shadows (Book 5)
The Last Run (Book 6)
Dark Corners (Book 7)
Ghost Operative (Book 8)

ALEX MASON THRILLERS
Odin (Book 1)
Ice Cold Spy (Book 2)
Mason's Law (Book 3)
Assets and Liabilities (Book 4)
Russian Roulette (Book 5)

Executive Order (Book 6)
Dead Man Talking (Book 7)
All The King's Men (Book 8)
Flashpoint (Book 9)
Brotherhood of the Goat (Book 10)
Dead Hot (Book 11)
Blood on Megiddo (Book 12)
Son of Hell (Book 13)

NOAH WOLF THRILLERS
Code Name Camelot (Book 1)
Lone Wolf (Book 2)
In Sheep's Clothing (Book 3)
Hit for Hire (Book 4)
The Wolf's Bite (Book 5)
Black Sheep (Book 6)
Balance of Power (Book 7)
Time to Hunt (Book 8)
Red Square (Book 9)
Highest Order (Book 10)
Edge of Anarchy (Book 11)
Unknown Evil (Book 12)
Black Harvest (Book 13)
World Order (Book 14)
Caged Animal (Book 15)
Deep Allegiance (Book 16)
Pack Leader (Book 17)
High Treason (Book 18)
A Wolf Among Men (Book 19)
Rogue Intelligence (Book 20)
Alpha (Book 21)

Rogue Wolf (Book 22)
Shadows of Allegiance (Book 23)
In the Grip of Darkness (Book 24)

SAM PRICHARD MYSTERIES
The Grave Man (Book 1)
Death Sung Softly (Book 2)
Love and War (Book 3)
Framed (Book 4)
The Kill List (Book 5)
Drifter: Part One (Book 6)
Drifter: Part Two (Book 7)
Drifter: Part Three (Book 8)
The Last Song (Book 9)
Ghost (Book 10)
Hidden Agenda (Book 11)

SAM AND INDIE MYSTERIES
Aces and Eights (Book 1)
Fact or Fiction (Book 2)
Close to Home (Book 3)
Brave New World (Book 4)
Innocent Conspiracy (Book 5)
Unfinished Business (Book 6)
Live Bait (Book 7)
Alter Ego (Book 8)
More Than It Seems (Book 9)
Moving On (Book 10)
Worst Nightmare (Book 11)
Chasing Ghosts (Book 12)
Serial Superstition (Book 13)

CHANCE REDDICK THRILLERS
Innocent Injustice (Book 1)
Angel of Justice (Book 2)
High Stakes Hunting (Book 3)
Personal Asset (Book 4)

CASSIE MCGRAW MYSTERIES
What Lies Beneath (Book 1)
Can't Fight Fate (Book 2)
One Last Game (Book 3)
Never Really Gone (Book 4)

ALSO BY BLAKE BANNER

Up to date books can be found at:
www.righthouse.com/blake-banner

ROGUE THRILLERS
Gates of Hell (Book 1)
Hell's Fury (Book 2)

ALEX MASON THRILLERS
Odin (Book 1)
Ice Cold Spy (Book 2)
Mason's Law (Book 3)
Assets and Liabilities (Book 4)
Russian Roulette (Book 5)
Executive Order (Book 6)
Dead Man Talking (Book 7)
All The King's Men (Book 8)
Flashpoint (Book 9)
Brotherhood of the Goat (Book 10)
Dead Hot (Book 11)
Blood on Megiddo (Book 12)
Son of Hell (Book 13)

HARRY BAUER THRILLER SERIES
Dead of Night (Book 1)
Dying Breath (Book 2)
The Einstaat Brief (Book 3)

Quantum Kill (Book 4)
Immortal Hate (Book 5)
The Silent Blade (Book 6)
LA: Wild Justice (Book 7)
Breath of Hell (Book 8)
Invisible Evil (Book 9)
The Shadow of Ukupacha (Book 10)
Sweet Razor Cut (Book 11)
Blood of the Innocent (Book 12)
Blood on Balthazar (Book 13)
Simple Kill (Book 14)
Riding The Devil (Book 15)
The Unavenged (Book 16)
The Devil's Vengeance (Book 17)
Bloody Retribution (Book 18)
Rogue Kill (Book 19)
Blood for Blood (Book 20)

DEAD COLD MYSTERY SERIES
An Ace and a Pair (Book 1)
Two Bare Arms (Book 2)
Garden of the Damned (Book 3)
Let Us Prey (Book 4)
The Sins of the Father (Book 5)
Strange and Sinister Path (Book 6)
The Heart to Kill (Book 7)
Unnatural Murder (Book 8)
Fire from Heaven (Book 9)
To Kill Upon A Kiss (Book 10)
Murder Most Scottish (Book 11)

The Butcher of Whitechapel (Book 12)
Little Dead Riding Hood (Book 13)
Trick or Treat (Book 14)
Blood Into Wine (Book 15)
Jack In The Box (Book 16)
The Fall Moon (Book 17)
Blood In Babylon (Book 18)
Death In Dexter (Book 19)
Mustang Sally (Book 20)
A Christmas Killing (Book 21)
Mommy's Little Killer (Book 22)
Bleed Out (Book 23)
Dead and Buried (Book 24)
In Hot Blood (Book 25)
Fallen Angels (Book 26)
Knife Edge (Book 27)
Along Came A Spider (Book 28)
Cold Blood (Book 29)
Curtain Call (Book 30)

THE OMEGA SERIES
Dawn of the Hunter (Book 1)
Double Edged Blade (Book 2)
The Storm (Book 3)
The Hand of War (Book 4)
A Harvest of Blood (Book 5)
To Rule in Hell (Book 6)
Kill: One (Book 7)
Powder Burn (Book 8)
Kill: Two (Book 9)
Unleashed (Book 10)

ABOUT US

Right House is an independent publisher created by authors for readers. We specialize in Action, Thriller, Mystery, and Crime novels.

If you enjoyed this novel, then there is a good chance you will like what else we have to offer! Please stay up to date by using any of the links below.

Join our mailing lists to stay up to date -->
righthouse.com/email
Visit our website --> righthouse.com
Contact us --> contact@righthouse.com

facebook.com/righthousebooks
x.com/righthousebooks
instagram.com/righthousebooks

www.ingramcontent.com/pod-product-compliance
Lightning Source LLC
Chambersburg PA
CBHW020410210626
46816CB00006BB/2218